Herbs and Homicide

Astoria Wright

Faerie Apothecary Mysteries
Book 1

Herbs and Homicide

Copyright © 2018 by Astoria Wright

Published by Novelwright Press, LLC
http://www.novelwright.com

Cover Art by Viyiwi
https://www.fiverr.com/viyiwi

First Round Editing by Tiffany Shand
https://eclipseediting.com

Final Editing by 529 Books
www.529books.com
Editors: Lisa Cerasoli and Adrian Muraro

Table of Contents

Moss Hill Island

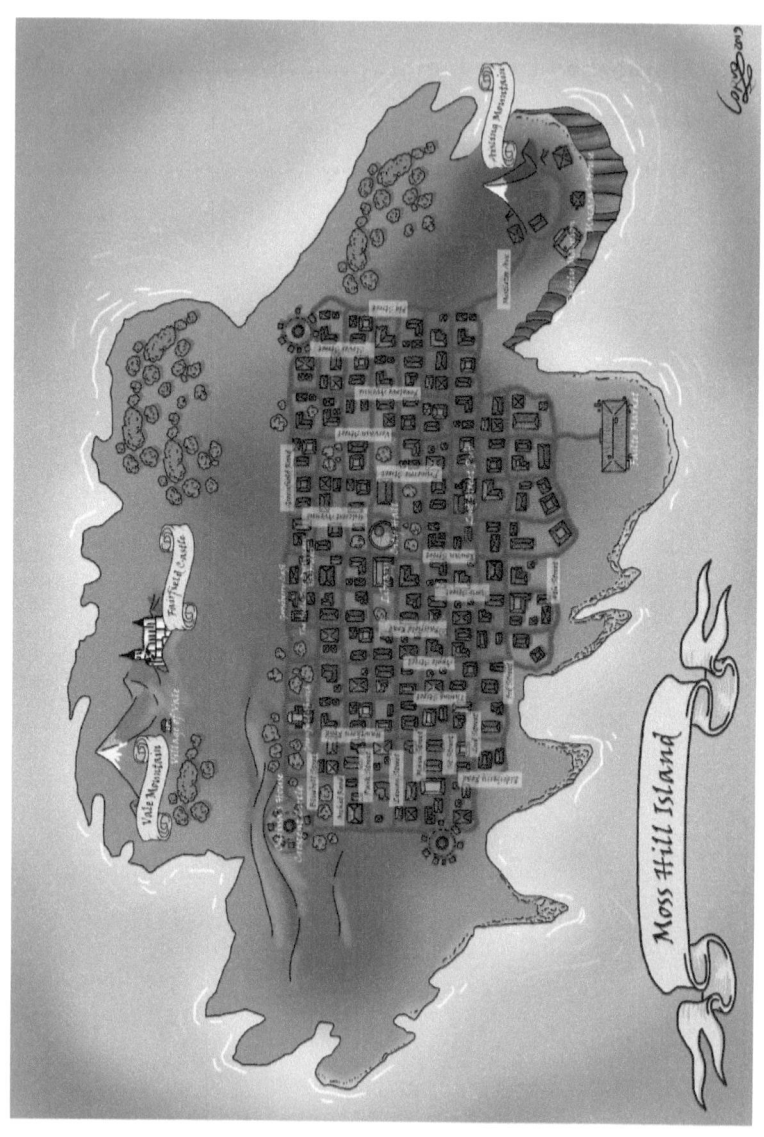

Chapter 1

Morning in Moss Hill

Perched above the pedals of her blue beach cruiser, Carissa Shea navigated the winding paths of the friendly neighborhood of Crescent Circle in the early morning hours. Her light pink blouse flared. The locket around her neck pressed against her chest in the wind. The red-haired, fair-skinned woman with the dark brown eyes and slightly pointed ears was unmistakably human and undeniably fae, depending on one's knowledge of the otherworldly people.

And no one knew the Otherworld better than the residents of Moss Hill. Mossies, as the people of this town on an island west of the UK called themselves, were the most diverse people the countries of the United Kingdom were not entirely aware existed. Their modest homes and shops with views of rolling green knolls sat snugly between two mountains. Each was a world of its own in more ways than one.

From the start of her daily routine, in the cozy cul-de-sac on the top of a hill, Carissa had a clear view of the western mountain. The forest and trees of Mount Vale were covered not just in moss but in faerie magic. Originating from hidden homes in the Vale woods, elves, sidhe, gnomes, sprites, brownies, and a host of other larger faeries, known as fae, were well known to the Mossies. Some even lived within the borders of town as neighbors and friends, as citizens, in fact, of Moss Hill. Even little ones like the tiny winged nature faeries, called sprites, lived in the gardens of their fae and human neighbors. Carissa passed a whole fluttering cloud of them just waking in the community garden as she exited Crescent Circle. This might just have looked like shimmering air to an untrained eye, but Cari waved as she rode by the flower-sized faeries.

The path at this point became one long stretch of pavement, aptly named Greenfield, surrounded by farmer's fields, blooming in the summer sun. The aroma of sweet corn mixed with the scent of saltwater that permeated the air on windy days like this one. It delighted her nose as she traveled through the quaint countryside.

A few meters down was a place where Greenfield diverged to a dirt path, leading toward Mount Vale, but Carissa wasn't going to the fae village today. She kept on course. Still, out of habit, she looked at the mountainside, curious whether her parents were home yet from their latest expedition. Her half-elfish eyes spotted the form of a woman coming down from the mountain. She was too far away to tell who or what type of fae, or even human, it was entering Moss Hill. Since it could've been any number of fae folks Carissa knew, she dismissed the sight as unimportant.

Inevitably, the road turned from smooth pavement to cobblestone, and Gorse Street came into view. Carissa veered right, stopping abruptly at the corner of Greenfield and Gorse. She hopped off the bicycle and walked alongside a red-brick building with full windows lining its front and side walls.

Gooseberry Bakery, with its open doors and sweet aroma wafting through the street, welcomed her as it did every other Saturday. The blueberry bagel for herself and lemon Danish for her assistant, as requested, made the perfect start to the last day of her workweek. She set her bicycle by a lamp post and secured it with a little elfish magic. Then she walked through the glass doors, over the checkered black and white flooring, past the red booths to the row of temptation under glass casing. The cashier, a sociable teen on her summer break, had anticipated her order. With no one in line, it was only a few minutes from paid to pastries in hand. Carissa thanked the girl and headed to the bright blue doors of the next building over.

The Seelie Tree Apothecary shop, open Monday through Saturday from 9:00 a.m. to 4:00 p.m., wasn't the newest or fanciest building in Moss Hill. Worn but well loved, the building had character—all the way down to its gray-tinted windows. Carissa knew every creaking sound, every item, and every regular customer to walk through.

The chime of the large silver bell overhead rang as Carissa passed through the entryway. With her pink tote on one shoulder, purse on the other and juggling the keys with the brown paper bags from Gooseberry Café in her hands, she maneuvered past the door and managed to turn on the lights. As always, the sight of the well-stocked rows of herbal tonics and healing teas welcomed her. She walked to the back counter and put down the items in her hands, then strolled to the short hallway to the right. The one and only room in the back served both as an office and a storeroom for additional stock, even though the space itself was minuscule for such purposes. Carissa placed her purse on the coatrack and heard the back door click open. It was followed by the soft footsteps of her assistant, Maren Raines.

"Morning! It's a beautiful day, isn't it?" Maren said, her wind whisked, ash-brown hair caught the corner of her mouth. She pulled it aside and brushed the strands back with her fingers so that the shoulder-length cut fell right into place. Carissa's long auburn waves never settled as easily. It was one of the many qualities Maren failed to see about herself. Despite her inability to accept praise, Maren's cheerful attitude wasn't unusual. Her lips tugged into an ever-increasing smile as she entered the room and set down her azure handbag on the stand beside Carissa's apple-red one.

"Someone is happy," Carissa observed. The two ladies exited the storeroom back to the counter, where Maren spotted the Gooseberry Bakery bags. She didn't wait for her boss to hand it over, immediately scooping it up.

"Mmm," Maren breathed in deeply, "it smells like three hundred calories for a taste of heaven: completely worth it."

Carissa shook her head. Maren's usual was about the same number of calories as Carissa's, the difference being the wrenching guilt that seemed to come only with Maren's order, regardless of whose turn it was to buy on any given Saturday. Carissa tried to reassure Maren that the weekly Danish wasn't the worst vice in the world, but Maren only ever responded in her sing-song voice, "Not everyone has elven genes to keep them young and fit, Cari." Never mind that both of them were only thirty.

Today Maren didn't seem as concerned. She bit happily into the lemon Danish, closing her eyes and giving a soft moan of delight. Setting the treat down on the bag, Maren smacked her hands together to get the crumbs off. Carissa resisted the urge to dust off the counter while her assistant was still eating.

"So, are you going to tell me what's got you in such a good mood?" Carissa said, tipping the cherry blossom tote and gently sliding the packages of herbs across the counter. She and Maren sorted them, some going in the large round herb baskets in the metal stands along the walls at the back of the shop, some in the shelves on the back wall directly behind them, and some would be put in the storeroom fridge for use later.

Maren hesitated, then spoke as she worked. "How would you feel if I maybe was dating someone whom you sort of went on a date with once?"

"Sort of? Oh, yes, the sort of date. I remember that."

"I'm serious. Would you mind if I were dating John, you know, Goodfellow?"

"I think I know his name. He hangs out around here enough. Come to think of it, I was wondering why he's been coming here every day. No one needs that many herbal supplements."

"Cari, will you answer my question, please? 'Cause I can't tell what you're really thinking when you're dodging like that."

Carissa gave an elfish smile, but her tone was warm. "I'm thinking I'm happy for my friend."

"Really?"

Cari set the last of the herbs on a shelf behind her and turned. She put both hands on the counter and gave her most earnest face to her friend. "Maren, I'm not pining after anyone. It was one date, and there's a reason why it ended early."

"You were attacked by a hoard of pixies," Maren said bluntly. The tension in her face had eased, but the still-furrowed brow told Cari her work reassuring her wasn't done.

Carissa grabbed the pink tote and dumped the remaining contents while saying as assertively as possible, "The pixies didn't kill our date, I assure you." She shrugged, picking up the books that had fallen to the counter. "We just weren't compatible. But I'm glad you are. I wish you luck, really."

She locked eyes with Maren and stressed the last word.

It seemed to relax Maren back into good spirits. "Thank you. We've only been on a few dates so far, and I wouldn't have even mentioned it except I'm starting to think there might be something there. Actually, John and I are going out again today. I wouldn't say it's a date this time, it may be a little unconventional." She rambled until Carissa raised her eyebrows. "Sorry, babbling."

"That's okay. Now, I'm curious. What's your big unconventional non-date going to be?"

"An old college friend of John's decided to take a trip out here and see the sights, so John promised he'd show her around, and he's invited me to come along."

"Her?"

Maren clucked her tongue. "It's not like that. They knew each other in grade school and met again in his last year of college. He doesn't know her all that well anymore. He thought her reaching out to him was a little odd, which is maybe part of the reason he wanted me along."

Carissa reserved her judgment and replied with only a, "Mmhm."

She grabbed the books and Maren reached for them, opening her mouth as if to make another argument. She quieted before even starting as she looked at the cover of the text in her hands. Tea and Roses, the title read.

"The poetry anthology? The cover came out nice." Maren's fingers traced the floral print of the first ever poetry anthology of Moss Hill's poetry club.

Carissa leaned with her elbows on the counter and one hand on her chin, smiling. "Nan's proud of it."

Carissa fully believed her grandmother was prouder of being the society's president than she was of being the Head Librarian of the Moss Hill Library for the last thirty-odd years. It was a close second, however. Nessa Shea, Nan to Carissa, was semi-retired but still worked at the information desk three days a week, enough to hear young Mossies' complaints about the library's outdated stacks and technology. She had taken it upon herself to publish the collection of poems and organize an event for tonight for the release as a fundraising campaign for her beloved workplace.

"It doesn't really go with the type of books we carry," Carissa looked past the aisles as if she could see the bookshelves at the windows carrying items on health and healing, "but I thought we could put a few in the front. Nan liked the idea of the Seelie Tree Apothecary being the only place for people to get an advanced copy."

Worry creased Maren's forehead. "I know I said I'd go to the poetry signing…."

Carissa waved off her angst. "It's fine. I completely understand. You go with John and have a good time." Then she added with faux seriousness, "Just make sure you sit between John and his friend wherever you go."

Maren rolled her eyes and made her way down the center row. Finished with the herbs, Carissa folded up the canvas bag and placed it on the shelves below the counter. Then she took a bite of the blueberry bagel. Delicious, as expected. The berries were juicy and tart, the bread crisp on the outside, fluffy on the inside. She closed her eyes and exhaled, enjoying the flavor.

Her attention turned next to tidying up the shop while she ate her breakfast. She wiped the surface of the tablet that served as their register and dusted the antique wood cashbox secured supernaturally to the counter, courtesy of the very little fae-magic Cari knew. By the time she finished the entire counter space, minus the area where Maren's half-eaten Danish lay, she was on the last bite of blueberry goodness. She moved on to other areas of the shop.

There was that little part of her that was a perfectionist, only about the store, of all things. She wanted every label frontward facing, shelves dusted, floor spic and span, so every part of a customer's experience was delightful. Even the crumbs of the bagel and the Gooseberry bag were neatly disposed of so that the only evidence of carbs left behind was the sweet aroma left in the air.

True, instead of thinking about work or savoring the scent of blueberry, a normal person might muse about their best friend's date with an old fling, but John was hardly that. He was new to Moss Hill, didn't understand the unusual relationship the humans here had with the Otherworld, and he definitely didn't understand her.

It made it awkward seeing him around town, especially since he was an investor who didn't work a typical day job and seemed to be in every corner of the island for her and Maren to bump into all the time. At first, when he began stopping by the apothecary shop with increasing frequency, Carissa dreaded the thought he might still be interested in her, but she quickly realized it was Maren who'd caught his eye.

And, why not? She had a girl-next-door quality to her that made her beautiful inside and out. She deserved to be happy.

John Goodfellow did strike Carissa as a bit more charismatic than she found appealing, but he was a tall drink of water, even if he wasn't Carissa's cup of tea. And though he wasn't a born and bred Mossie, he was learning to blend in with Moss Hill culture well enough.

"Hey, Cari?" Maren called from another aisle.

Carissa's face flushed a little, realizing she was pondering John and Maren's relationship, despite deciding before that she wouldn't give it another thought. "Yeah?" Cari replied.

"Could you take the Otherworld today? I don't think I can handle old Miss Morgan."

"Why? She's not coming in today, is she?"

"She said, 'The day after that apothecary mixes her tonics,' so it's 'fresh' and not 'musty and old.' She's just so mean. Are you sure she's not unseelie?"

Miss Morgan was rude, curt, regularly made comments about her disproval of most people and often argued about the stock they should keep in the apothecary. While it was annoying, it didn't make her one of the evil-natured faeries. Plus, Carissa had to admit there had been times when Miss Morgan's tonic recipes or insight on people's purchases were spot-on. No dark faerie would be helpful like that.

"Maren!" Carissa warned. Unseelie or not, making any faerie mad was a bad decision for a human. "You know they can hear through the veil if they want to. Be careful with your wording. You wouldn't want to make a brownie mad at you."

"All right, sorry." Maren held her hands up defensively. "Can you please take her order today?"

"Yes, but you owe me. And remember, to owe a human is one thing, to owe a faerie is another." Carissa gave a devious smile.

Maren laughed. With relief in her eyes, the crinkles around her mouth deepened as her lips curled upwards.

Carissa turned to the shelves behind her. "Did I prepare Miss Morgan's order yet?" she inquired to no one in particular. Maren had gone back to reorganizing the nutrition books at the front of the store as Cari searched. She either didn't hear her boss or didn't know whether the apothecary was genuinely asking or talking to herself.

"Ah, here it is," Carissa announced. She tried to prepare orders every Friday, for the next week just so she could restock on weekends in case she didn't have the necessary items for the tonics. "I remember now," she mused loud enough for Maren to hear, "I was distracted by your boyfriend chatting away, keeping you from helping me."

"I'd apologize, but I don't control him," Maren dramatized the words. Cari imagined she was curving her shoulders forward with her hands on her heart for added flair. "It's not my fault if he can't resist seeing me."

Carissa chuckled. Then, she took her locket out from the chain on her neck. Two silver circles were set together, one hollow holding one with glass and herbs in the middle. She spun the inner one, turning it thrice. The world became still. The metaphysical veils parted for her to step into the Otherworld. This really looked like nothing more than a woman disappearing in full view. To Cari, it looked like fog forming and then vanishing all around her. The world took on a strange hue, indescribably brighter and dimmer at once, like a dream. A bit unsettling, maybe, but any Mossie who'd seen the Otherworld was used to it. She opened the shop by magic, breaking the seal on the front doors and lighting the sign with a flick of her hand.

A few words in old druidic next allowed her to see into both worlds at once. Maren, being only fae-touched, meaning that she had interacted with the fae before but wasn't genetically related to any of them, couldn't do what Carissa could as half-fae. With skill and much practice, Maren probably could learn the trick of it, but she'd still need to borrow fae magic to do it. Instead, Carissa saw her walk to the door to unlock it from her world on the human side of things.

"Let me guess," Maren said, "You came in through the front this morning? You forgot to lock the door."

Carissa's chin swayed in the tiniest display of disapproval. She wasn't exactly spying on her assistant since Maren knew she could see her. She was only watching to see if Maren needed any help. But Maren talked to her all the time when they were in opposite sides of reality, knowing full well her boss could hear her. Carissa hated that. She'd told Maren more than once she'd look crazy if anyone caught her rambling to an invisible person.

"They all know we're talking to each other," Maren responded.

She failed to consider that not everyone who came into the Seelie Tree was a Mossie. Tourists often found the charm of an old rustic apothecary shop of interest on their excursions around Moss Hill. They didn't believe in half the items they carried but found them intriguing nonetheless. An assistant conversing with the air, however, went beyond intrigue toward lunacy. If they saw that, they might not care to stay and shop.

The bells chimed above the door frame. The light, airy sound resonated melodiously in the Otherworld—as it could only sound in the realm of the fae.

"Good morning," Carissa called out to the customer. A very short woman with sharp eyes and a cane came hobbling up the center aisle. The faded black dress she wore dragged across the floor and the long sleeves looked odd in the summer. Her countenance was clearly recognizable as a brownie, the small-statured fae who lived with Mossies and helped them with chores, except they were always kind and she was…Miss Morgan.

"What's good about it?" asked the old woman.

"Miss Morgan, lovely to see you."

"S'not lovely, you liar. You've been arguing with pink-ears about me. I could hear you a mile away."

"Now, Miss Morgan. It's not nice to be listening in on conversations when you're not in the room."

The brownie stopped and leaned forward. Her walking stick wobbled. She twitched her ears and pulled her head back with one eye rising considerably higher than the other. If Carissa were full-human, she wouldn't get away with talking to a fae like that, but her half-elf status protected her from Miss Morgan's wrath. The old brownie finally made her way to the counter.

"I'll be needing my usual order."

Carissa turned to the shelves and picked out the tonic—a yellowish tincture. A flick of a finger against the glass caused the liquid to swirl to a bright green color with a subtle sparkling glow.

"Here you are. That'll be four coins."

The customer put a pendant and scarf on the counter. The necklace was beautiful. It had the insignia of a tree delicately carved onto the surface. It was likely expensive but probably stolen from some human neighbor—likely the Everlys, whom Miss Morgan was "staying with" uninvited at the moment. They were rich enough to afford it, but it wasn't hers to trade.

The bell rang as another customer walked in. Carissa's eyes darted upward. It was a regular, Sal. The elfkin, a helper to the elves, was upbeat as always, his sharp nose and pointed ears were accentuated by a wide, outgoing smile. He waved from the door.

"Hello, Carissa!"

According to faerie tradition, it would be equally rude not to finish the conversation with her current customer as it would be to ignore Sal's greeting. It was a delicate balancing act that Carissa managed quite well on a near-daily basis.

"I cannot barter, Miss Morgan. Please look in your purse for coins while I greet Sal," Carissa said, then she looked up at her next customer and called out with equal cheer. "Good morning, Sal."

Miss Morgan grumpily rummaged through her purse, looking for payment while Carissa maintained her warm demeanor. The door chimed again. It was the low din of the shop bells in the human world. The sound was accompanied by a greeting from Maren. Out of the corner of her eye,

Carissa could see a man she'd never met before. He wore a hooded jacket. Strangely, he had a presence that felt otherworldly. There was a touch of magic about him.

A druid, perhaps? Fae-touched, possibly? Or was he like her, half-fae? No, that wasn't it. But what was it, then?

She couldn't pay it much mind at the moment. The brownie threw four coins roughly on the table and grabbed the bottle of tonic from her hands. A bit annoyed, Carissa kept her calm demeanor.

"Thank you and have a good day," she said.

Miss Morgan made no reply. She merely turned and took a swig of the tonic, then made her way to the other end of the shop.

"Miss Morgan's in a happy mood today, wouldn't you say?" Sal bounded over.

Carissa smiled, both because she was glad to see him and because of his lighthearted attitude.

"And how are you today, Sal? Are the elf-folk treating you nicely?"

"Can't complain. Master Rolin did send me with a list." He handed her a folded parchment with his hurried scrawling barely readable going down it.

She held the note up and squinted. "Bluebell, elderberry, mistletoe, heather…is there a party going on that I don't know about?"

Sal rested an elbow on the counter, bringing him considerably lower than his tall, lanky height. "The whole of Moss Hill is invited, fae and fae-touched only, I mean."

"What's it for? It can't be a solstice celebration. That won't be for a few more months."

"No, not that." His eyes twinkled.

"You want me to guess?" Carissa was used to the fae mind by now. Riddles and games were second nature to many of them. It was like a test one had to continually take to pass muster. Sometimes it could be exhausting.

She started to think of possible events. It was August, past the summer solstice and far too early for winter. Was there a human holiday coming soon? The fae of Moss Hill had taken to celebrating human holidays a century ago, but Carissa could think of none that were approaching soon. Then, she realized that in the absence of a holiday, the next celebratory event the fae loved most was love itself: a wedding. Not Sal's wedding, he was a confirmed bachelor. The elfkin wasn't here for himself anyway, he'd said his master had sent him today. That must mean one of the Elvin children, an older one at least around a hundred years, might have just gotten engaged.

"Is Hela getting married?" She guessed the eldest daughter to be about the right age.

Sal didn't have time to respond. A sharp cry came from the front of the store. Carissa froze. Sal turned around.

Both were unprepared for what they saw next.

Chapter 2

A Mossie Murdered?

Carissa hadn't noticed Miss Morgan was still in the store. Or rather, maybe she had seen her skimming the bookshelves but let it pass out of her conscious awareness. Whatever the case, she was startled when she heard the strangled outcry coming from the other side of the shop. The sound of distress was followed by a clattering of books and smashing of vials. Sal sprang to the front of the store. Carissa had to swerve around the counter, and so she lagged. When she passed the end of the center isle's shelving, she saw it. There, in front of the bookcase just to the left of the door, lay Miss Morgan.

She was sprawled out with one hand over her head. Several books—from *Healing with Herbs* to the ironic *Secrets to a Long Life*—had fallen from the shelf next to her. The vial of herbal tonic Carissa had given her lay open in her hand, spilling out onto the floor.

Sal lifted Miss Morgan's head and put an ear to her mouth. Sal's words barely registered; something about her breathing being raspy. Miss Morgan was unconscious, but at least she was still alive.

Herbs and Homicide

Carissa's eyes glided to the man leaving the store. The tall, black-haired man was in the human world with Maren, so why was he looking at Miss Morgan? His hand was on the door, and all the rest of him was poised to leave, except he didn't. Instead, he stared at them, then turned his head toward Carissa in unnatural slow motion. He looked at her for a long second, directly in her eyes.

There was no malice in his expression, but the simple fact he could see them was enough to cause alarm bells to go off in her mind. He opened the door, held it longer than he should have, and left without so much as a backward glance. Now alone with Sal and Miss Morgan, Carissa raced over to them.

What had she been thinking, wasting time like that? Though she wasn't a doctor, she was the apothecary in the shop. That made her the most qualified to help in this situation.

"Is she still breathing?" Carissa asked.

"No, no. I don't think she is." Sal looked up with a sense of desperation in his eyes that unnerved her. He didn't have the skill or magic to heal, and his helplessness only added to the weight on her shoulders.

"Stand back," she said.

Sal gently laid Miss Morgan's head to rest on the floor and walked a few paces to watch from the corner.

Carissa wasn't as good with elf-light as she wished, but she chanted a few words and moved her palms in opposite circles facing each other. Swirling the light in her hands until it brightened, she knelt over Miss Morgan and centered her hands above her heart. The energy surging through her detected a darkness in the brownie's lungs—poison. She could see it now with her eyes better than an X-ray.

She had several items in the shop that could work as an antidote, but without knowing exactly which poison it was, she wouldn't be able to counteract it. She'd have to try using her elf-light magic. The problem was, she'd only ever used it for detecting illnesses and creating herbal remedies. She knew elves used the light magic to heal, but her training as an apothecary had been learned among humans. Her knowledge of elvish light was limited: another drawback of her parents' constant traveling. She wasn't even sure of her limits and hoped she had enough ability to heal her now.

Carissa closed her eyes and concentrated. She could feel the soft heat of the light at her fingertips expanding. Could it be working? The energy flowed until a tension pushed at her hands. She opened her eyes. The light was turning black, growing, then it dissipated. Everything disappeared. She tried again, calling the light out from within her, but there was nothing for it to detect in the body. Miss Morgan, if she had still been alive, was gone now.

Carissa snapped back to her feet. She stared at the brownie's body in shock. Already the hands and feet were becoming taut like wood. How could this have happened? She retrieved the bottle of tonic from her open hand and replaced the cork. As she knelt, she closed Miss Morgan's eyes in peaceful rest.

"We have to call the sidhe guard," Sal said softly. Carissa nodded, still too shaken to say anything.

Sal left, presumably to fetch the local faerie authority on duty this morning. A moment passed with the vial in her hands. She gripped it with no awareness of her knuckles turning white. A single phrase repeated in her mind: *How could this have happened?*

Chapter 3

A Vial Realization

The sidhe (shee) were not an agreeable people. The oldest of the faerie races considered non-sidhe beneath them in beauty, wisdom, and nearly every aspect except humor. Some feelings were simply useless, according to them. The sidhe guards in front of her definitely shared that mindset.

The leader she recognized but couldn't quite recall his name. He must have been newly promoted to first in command. His bronze badge glinted with an immaculate shine as he knelt over Miss Morgan's body.

"And you used fae magic to heal her?" The flecks of gold in his brown eyes blazed.

"I tried," Carissa said. This evoked a grimace on his obnoxiously chiseled face.

He rose and walked with them toward the back of the store. The rest of the guards surrounded Miss Morgan, casting spells to examine the evidence. Carissa could see Maren in the human world, oblivious to any disturbance.

"Did you attempt to find a cause before starting to heal her?" The main sidhe's contempt was unmistakable, pointing out the glaringly obvious like she knew nothing of healing.

Varick. That was his name. She recalled his surly demeanor from a previous encounter when she'd lost one of the nature faeries from her garden. She had to bite her tongue. This was about Miss Morgan, not her.

"Of course," she said. The guard stared until Cari realized he was waiting for her to clarify. "Oh," she cleared her throat. "Um, it seemed like poison."

"Seemed like?"

"OK, it was poison."

"What kind?"

"I didn't have time to find that out."

"Mm-hmm. What did you do next?"

"I tried to heal her with the elf-light."

Varick grunted a half-chortle half-snicker that made her want to scream in frustration. She kept calm. She wasn't a banshee after all.

She admonished herself with a frown. She shouldn't think ill of the ban sidhe. The widowed sidhe couldn't help their distress. And such wry humor, even in thought, wasn't appropriate given the circumstances.

She watched the sidhe retrieve a small notepad from his hands, a self-inking feather-pen scribbled words with his left hand onto a fresh page. His ear twitched as if he knew she was watching. It was pointier than Carissa's, naturally, and more so than any elf's she'd seen before. That made it snootier somehow.

"So, you gave her a vial, she drank it, then she collapsed, and you used the elf-light on her." He said the word elf-light with a heavy dose of skepticism as if it wasn't a real word. "Then she died?" The way the guard recounted events sounded more like an accusation than a summary.

"Sir, um…" Sal intervened.

"Varick." The sidhe gave him his name.

"Varick, I was here the whole time. Carissa did everything she could to save her. She's a wonderful apothecary. She's always helping people. Why, Miss Morgan was rude as can be to her, and Carissa only ever responded kindly."

"She was rude to her, hmm?"

"Oh yes, she was always so ru—"

"Sal!" Cari's eyes flared with her tone. She could see the look on the sidhe's face changing from slight skepticism to full-blown suspicion. Sal was making things worse, and she'd only exacerbated the problem with her exclamation.

She tried a gentler approach. "Sir, uh, Varick," Carissa put as much respect into her tone as possible. "What happens now?"

"We'll take Miss Morgan and do a recasting to determine what poison, or magic, she has in her system." His tone dripped with disgust. "We'll find out what happened, you can be sure." He turned to leave.

Carissa's face fell. There was no mistaking this was murder. But how? How could something like this happen in her shop? She pictured the strange man who fled. There was no obvious way for him to have poisoned Miss Morgan, but, then again, she hadn't been watching him the whole time. Every piece of information might help the investigation. She called Varick back. The sidhe didn't hide his annoyance as he meandered back to the counter. With Varick looking at her straight on, she stumbled a bit as she spoke.

"There's something else you should know." Nervous, she swallowed her fear and told him, "There was a man here around the same time. He was in the human world, but he had a faerie presence. I don't know how to describe it. He acted like he could see and hear what was going on, but he didn't do anything to help. He looked right at me and just walked out."

The sidhe's expression was unchanging. "Did you see this man?" he asked Sal.

Poor Sal looked as if he didn't know what to do. Fear and confusion were etched on his face. He stammered, "I, um, well I wasn't looking in the human world, but if Cari says he was there, then I'm sure he was."

Carissa debated telling him about Maren. She would be able to support Cari's statement. As much as the sidhe loathed certain faerie races, they were especially unfriendly toward humans. Still, she might need to risk it.

"I have an assistant in the human world—" she began.

"We won't need any help from a human." Varick turned to the other guards, who were now taking Miss Morgan's body out of the apothecary shop. One of them gave him a look. He walked over. He said something and handed his superior the vial. Varick held it up to the light. Then he handed it back to the guard, who placed it in a leather bag.

Varick's eyes pierced right into Carissa's core as he said, "Don't think of fleeing anywhere until this is done. We wouldn't want to cast a binding on you unless we have to."

Carissa's eyes rounded to massive orbs. A binding? Was she really a suspect now?

The sidhe left without another word.

Sal turned to her with pleading eyes. "Carissa, I'm so sorry. I hope I didn't get you into any trouble."

"It's all right," Carissa replied, hoping that it was. "Look, you should go on home. I'll give you the materials on your list and close up shop, okay?" She gave him a half-hearted smile, which he accepted with one of his own.

On his way out, he flashed her a grin, adding, "By the way, you were right. It is a wedding. I'll give Hela your good wishes." Bags in hand, he pushed the door open with a foot and bounded out, leaving her to close for the rest of the afternoon. He'd probably meant to cheer her up with the last statement, but it was hard to think about a wedding on the heels of what they'd just witnessed.

Carissa waited until Maren had finished serving a few customers, then she phased out of the Otherworld and locked behind the existing customers. She was too put off to keep the store open in either world today. She didn't want Maren here alone in the store either, at least not until she had a chance to wrap her head around what had happened. Maren had nearly dropped the last of her lemon Danish all over the counter upon hearing the news.

"Miss Morgan's dead?" She put a hand to her mouth. "Oh my god, that's awful! I mean, I didn't like her, but dead?" Slowly, her hand dropped back to the counter, lingering on the Danish. She picked it up with a sour face and walked away with one last thought: "I wish I could say I can't believe it."

Maren's comment perplexed Carissa, who'd been clutching the counter as if it were steadying the sick feeling in her stomach. She let go and followed her assistant to the back room. Maren dumped the half-eaten Danish into the trash as Carissa asked, "What do you mean?"

Maren shrugged and ripped a paper towel off of the roll by the cleaning supplies. "No one liked her." That much was obvious. Carissa hugged her elbows and leaned against the wall, thinking. Could anyone really dislike Miss Morgan enough to want her dead? Carissa wasn't an inspector, but she was reasonably sure annoyance didn't qualify as a motive for murder.

When Maren walked back out, Cari composed herself with a breath. She reached for the mop. Carissa had to clear up the mess, whether she wanted to or not. She paused before making her way to the front of the store. At the counter, Maren had pulled up the stool neither of them ever used and sat with her arms contracted around herself. She appeared deep in thought. Her face was downcast. A shadow played over her features. When she did look at Carissa again, concern tugged at her lips and eyes.

"Maren, is there something you're not telling me?" Carissa asked.

Maren relaxed her arms and pulled back her shoulders as if deciding to be brave. "Did you see the man who came in here earlier?" Carissa nodded. She knew exactly who Maren meant. "There was something strange about him. He wasn't rude or anything, he just gave me the oddest feeling, like he was carrying a shadow on him."

"I know. I felt it too." She recalled him looking at her just before he left. His pale skin, ice blue eyes, and dark clothing all looked sinister. The hooded jacket had covered his head, but she'd noted a few out of place strands of black.

"Did the customer look familiar to you?"

Surprise lit up Maren's eyes like a light bulb. "Yes. Now that you mention it, he did." The two thought a moment. If Maren recalled where she'd seen him from, she didn't mention it. It wasn't coming to Carissa, either.

"Do you remember what he ordered?" Carissa asked.

Maren looked over the receipts logged on the tablet. "Thyme, primrose, St. John's wort, ash bark." She gasped and looked up. "And foxglove. Do you think—?"

"No," Carissa cut her off. "There's no way he could've administered it. Foxglove needs to be ingested to be poisonous, and there was no way he could've given it to Miss Morgan. As much as he may have seemed dangerous, I don't think he killed her."

"Then how?"

"I don't know."

Another moment passed in silence. Maren flicked through the table, presumably trying to jog her memory of the strange customer. Carissa leaned on the mop, trying to determine how such a poisoning could have happened in the Seelie Tree Apothecary. Finally, Cari snapped out of her blank stare and spoke.

"No use sticking around here. You go, I'll clean up."

"Isn't it a crime scene?"

"The sidhe already did their analysis. They won't bother coming back once they've completed a sweep of the site." She recalled from past experience the sidhe believed in doing things once and flawlessly, though Carissa didn't always agree with their definition of perfect. Many elves she knew felt the same way.

Maren relented. "Are you sure you'll be all right?"

"I'll be fine." Carissa tried to sound confident. She reiterated she was perfectly fine—but inside she was far from it.

She mopped the doorway, sweeping on automatic. A dozen thoughts vied for attention. The first was that she knew for certain the man who'd been there earlier had seen Miss Morgan. Images of the brownie came to mind. She felt her face grow hot as she stood, holding the mop. Of all her customers, she knew the least about Miss Morgan. But the old brownie had helped her in the past. She may have been rough around the edges, but she wasn't all bad. There might have even been a time in her life when she was kinder. Carissa closed her eyes. Her stomach knotted with guilt. She couldn't have saved her, she knew that, but she might just need someone to convince her of that fact.

Just as vivid was the image of that man's face. That face was familiar. Moss Hill was a small town, and though they had their fair share of tourists, none looked quite like him. Nor did any have a hint of being fae-touched like he did. He had to be a Mossie.

Disregarding his look, Mossies often did buy ingredients to keep up good relations with the faerie folk around the area. What he'd ordered made sense if one thought about it that way. Thyme and primrose for peering into the Otherworld—if properly used—they could help one to see the fae. Ash bark could be used in wand making or old spells, though no one used those anymore except mages and there were few of them left. Foxglove was an intriguing choice. Of course, it could be used as a poison. But, it could also be used in talismans, for protection, as could St. John's wort. The list wasn't necessarily suspicious. It wasn't fair for her to judge this person she had never actually met. He could be a harmless bystander, even if he had seen the turn of events this morning. But then, who could see a thing like that and walk away?

Suddenly, she realized that she was cleaning in the wrong realm. The human world was not where she ought to be cleaning. Carissa used the faerie glass locket to re-enter the Otherworld. The store seemed sadder and quieter. She breathed deeply. She should finish the mopping and get home as soon as possible. She hesitated to mop the scene of the crime but realized that she already had done so, in the human world at least.

Now, she could see streaks on the floor in this world, too. It wasn't entirely unusual. Things from one world often did seep into the other. What was unusual was the dark streak in one particular place on the floor.

She leaned toward it. It was a solitary black spot on the wood. This was no ordinary knot. What had made that mark?

She stepped back and pictured the scene. The vial in Miss Morgan's hand, the one containing the tonic; it had spilled from her hand when she'd collapsed. It would have fallen directly on that spot.

Carissa knelt. The concoction should not have produced any kind of reaction with the soapy water. She used her elf-light, hovering over the mark with her hand. It deepened in the shade like before, just like the poison. She gasped and stood. Whatever poison it was that had killed Miss Morgan, it was in the tonic.

Chapter 4

Poised for Poison

Carissa had barely finished mopping up the mess of tonic when she heard a tapping on the glass at the front of the shop. In the human world again, she figured it might be a customer wondering why the shop was closed, but a glance at the window revealed an altogether different visitor. She sighed.

There was Barnaby, dressed in a shamrock green suit, holding his cap in his hands, peering into the window. His bulbous nose was pressed against the glass and his pointed ears stuck out sideways. The stout leprechaun waved as she approached the door.

"Hello, Barn—"

"Is it true?" Barnaby's beady eyes looked up at her. "I saw the guard outside the door this morning and I had to run out of my shop to see for myself." His fae clothing and shoe shop, Barnaby's, existed in the Otherworld only, in dual existence with a haberdashery in the human world called Harbridge's. The building faced directly across the cobblestone street from the Seelie Tree Apothecary, so, of course, he would have noticed three sidhe in full blazing blue uniforms outside her shop. "Is Miss Morgan really dead?" He stroked his reddish-brown beard.

He wasn't asking because he cared for the old brownie, Carissa knew that much. He was one of the biggest gossips in either world. Whatever she told him she could be sure it would be spread throughout town before sunset.

Still, she couldn't lie. All of Moss Hill would find out eventually, probably from Barnaby and whether she told him.

"Yes, she's gone." She didn't know what else to say and wasn't about to elaborate.

"Well, how did she—what on earth—what do you think killed her?" His string of half-sentences showed Carissa how shaken he really was. She didn't blame him. It was far less common to hear about a fae death than that of a human, though both were equally tragic. She didn't know what more she should add, though, especially since the sidhe had just begun their investigation.

"Sorry, Barnaby, if you don't mind, it's been a very long morning, and I'd rather not talk about it."

"Of course." The leprechaun frowned. "I understand completely." His sinking shoulders said otherwise. "But just tell me this before you go." He stood on his tiptoes. His height discrepancy with humans was never so obvious as when he did this. "Do you think she was murdered?"

Carissa felt a chill run down her spine. Maren might have hinted at it. Varick had practically accused her of it. The poison had proved it. But hearing the actual word "murder" made it real.

Her mouth hung open, struggling to decide what words to form. If she confirmed it, there'd be talk all over town that would lead to speculation she'd rather not have about her shop. Furthermore, since she now knew it was her tonic that contained the poison, what could she say? Well, Miss Morgan was poisoned, and the poison came from something I gave her, but I didn't kill her…. That would make her a suspect in town even before the sidhe investigation had officially begun.

"I really couldn't say," she answered. She was never so elf-like as when she lied. Elves could only ever tell half-truths, but they were good at those. "I'm sure that sidhe guard will be able to tell us in a day or two."

The leprechaun didn't look convinced but backed down anyway. If he knew his elves, Barnaby wouldn't get a straight answer out of her unless she wanted to give it. He replaced his green cap on his head.

"Naturally, well, this must have been a harrowing event for you. I'll let you be off then and bid you a good day—a better one than it's been so far, that is." Barnaby swiveled around to the door, disappearing from human sight before it closed.

Carissa didn't care to see if a crowd had formed in the Otherworld or to hear what anyone there might be saying. She tucked the faerie glass locket under her blouse and turned away from the door.

Instead, she retrieved her tote and grabbed her mug from the countertop. With the shop clean and closed, Carissa rode her bicycle down the cobblestone streets to the paved road overlooking patches of wildflowers and farmers' fields. She walked her bicycle up the last half mile as Crescent Circle came into view. She was stopped just beside the community garden by a pack of flustered neighbors.

"Carissa, do you know who's speaking to your gran at this very moment?" the rotund man in the brown pantsuit asked without waiting. "The mayor!" Mr. Harbridge was beside himself. Having the mayor in his alley might normally have delighted a man like this small business owner, but the haberdasher turned redder as he spoke and twisted his hat in his hands like it was his own neck he was wringing.

"Mr. Larke says there's been a murder!" Mrs. Alcott proclaimed. Holding the giant clippers in her hands made her statement even more dramatic.

But Mrs. Harbridge's flair for drama exceeded her neighbor's. "Oh, Timothy, thank goodness you were home today!" Mr. Harbridge put his arm around her, though she pulled away quick enough to tend to her oversized sunhat as it fluttered on her head. Carissa suspected her exaggerated movements were more to blame for its unsteadiness than the wind. She nearly matched her husband's shade, though, to be fair, even with her sunhat she burned easily on her days in the shared garden.

"Naturally, we were scared for you." The clippers wobbled in Mrs. Alcott's gloved hands. Was she even scheduled to tend the crops today? Carissa thought not.

The three looked at the apothecary, finally waiting for her to speak. Carissa kicked open the bike stand, buying time to think of what to say. Hopefully, something reassuring would flow out of her mouth.

"Please don't be alarmed. A brownie did pass away, but you have nothing to worry about." She didn't have her grandmother's way with words. By the looks on their faces, she wasn't easing anyone's mind. She continued, "The fae are investigating, but there's no reason to believe this will affect the humans of Moss Hill." Carissa hoped that was good enough, but apparently, it didn't suffice.

"But who was it?" Mr. Harbridge asked. They all leaned toward her, long-faced and frightened. She almost believed they were asking out of genuine concern. But this second bout of questioning with her neighbors was harder than the first with Barnaby.

She swallowed the lump rising in her throat and answered. It was strange how a brownie known for her unpleasantness was so widely and so differently grieved. The two women wailed tears that Carissa highly suspected were fake.

But Mr. Harbridge's reaction seemed sincere. "How was Barnaby?" he asked. "Did he see it happen?"

"No," Carissa assured, but she tilted her head, wondering why he was concerned for the leprechaun.

"Poor Barn, he must be devastated," Mr. Harbridge said.

Carissa didn't quite see why. By all accounts, Barnaby didn't like Miss Morgan. He avoided her when he could and was often on the other end of her stick when she did catch wind of him nearby. If anything, he seemed afraid of her.

Herbs and Homicide

With the mayor supposedly waiting, she'd didn't have time to ponder Barnaby's relationship with Miss Morgan. She politely excused herself and kept onward toward home.

Sure enough, the mayor's chauffeur stood at the edge of her yard when she approached. Cameron Larke was not as bad as Barnaby, but he was a close second for nosiest Mossie. He might have made first place if Barn hadn't moved down the mountain to town. How the mayor could choose to keep him by his side was unfathomable! Though, if she thought about it, it was probably his penchant for knowing the town gossip, in both fae and human worlds, that made the mayor want him in his employ as a chauffeur. After all, a mayor must be informed.

Cameron leaned back with his arms on the gate, no doubt trying for a listen at the closest window without breaking the mayor's orders to stay with the car. The metal squeaked as he lifted his tall, wiry person off it. "Carissa, let me be the first to say that no one who knows you even remotely suspects you had any involvement in Miss Morgan's death." Comforting, especially since he had felt a need to say those words aloud.

"Thank you, Cameron."

She felt a tension rising in her chest. Her emotions were easier to control in front of Barnaby and even Mrs. Alcott and the Harbridges, but Cam she'd known since they were kids. Despite his ill-chosen words, she knew his intention was genuinely kind. Her voice was stuck in her throat now and a weight clamped down on her chest. She wasn't sure what she was feeling exactly, something between fear and grief.

She wasn't disdainful of emotion like the sidhe but instead, like the elves, she was more inclined to try to avoid the negative ones. When she was steady enough to speak, she asked, "How exactly did you hear about it?" Her voice wavered slightly against her will. She hoped he hadn't heard it.

"As you know, my great—"

"—great grandmother on your father's side was a water faerie, I know. You must have repeated that a hundred times when we were in school." Impatience: that would be her avoidance of fear.

"A Gragedd Annwn. Not all water faeries are the same."

She cleared her throat, both annoyed by his correction and by her own previous near-display of anxiety. "Please just answer my question, Cam." Now she was legitimately at exasperation. She bit her lip in an effort to bite her tongue.

"I was getting to it." Annoyance seemed to flush his cheeks, but he continued, "The family whom Miss Morgan was staying with, the Everlys, are also descendants of a Gragedd Annwn, different lake, though. They're good friends with my parents ever since they discovered their similar backgrounds." He could've just said they were friends without the fae-related history, but Carissa didn't feel like arguing that point. "Anyway, a fae in town saw the sidhe guards and found out it was a brownie who had died. They told another brownie, who broke the news to Mrs. Everly, who told my mother just about an hour ago. Naturally, the brownies are scared witless, thinking someone might be killing them off."

Carissa didn't need multiple guesses to figure out the fae in town was Barnaby. She didn't know a single brownie who liked Miss Morgan, but she could understand why they would be scared. In her position, she didn't know what she could do to alleviate their fears.

"It's a terrible shame, though, with everything the Everlys have gone through," Cameron said.

"What do you mean? What have they gone through?" Carissa pushed her hair back from the breeze picking up around them.

He stepped closer, saying in hushed tones, "Last year their eldest son came back from a business trip, sick with pneumonia. He'd been neglecting his health for a while. Doctors said there was nothing that could be done for him. He died in December."

Carissa closed her eyes as realization swept over her. "Jane Everly. I remember now. Jane joined Nan's poetry group in the literary society in February. She mentioned there had been a death in Jane's family. The writing helped her grieve."

Cam nodded.

"So that's two deaths in the family?" She considered the implications. Was someone targeting the Everlys? Pneumonia didn't seem like a method for murder. Was it a strange coincidence? Either way, someone had definitely targeted Miss Morgan.

"Mysterious, isn't it?" Cam's soft-spoken response was unexpected. She even stepped back involuntarily. "Didn't mean to scare you," he added. His hands drew upward.

She put a hand to her chest. Startled, maybe, but scared? No. He had scared her earlier, not now. Just now, he'd given her something else to think about. Distractions were good. She could deal with those.

She felt herself relaxing. She didn't mean to be so annoyed with Cameron. Even if he was a gossip or had a little bravado to him, he was a harmless one and never spread a rumor he thought was untrue or unkind. She softened.

"Why is the mayor here, though? Why not at the Seelie Tree or trying to get ahold of the fae leaders?"

Cam's expression transformed from solemn to grave by the shadow passing over his face. "He did, Cari. I wanted to speak with you alone before you spoke to the mayor. There's a bit of suspicion about it having happened in the apothecary shop and some talk that it was after Miss Morgan had drunk a tonic from you."

Cari's face froze, trying not to show emotion, though the fear was back, full force this time. He wasn't revealing anything she hadn't already discovered. She knew it was only a matter of time before the sidhe discovered it too. This was precisely what she had been worried about. Whoever had planned the murder wanted it to look like Carissa was guilty. Cameron's brows slanted downward sympathetically.

"You don't need to explain anything to me, Carissa. I know you couldn't have done anything wrong, but I'm cautioning you not to tell the mayor any more than you have to. He likes you well enough, but he's more interested in keeping good relations between Moss Hill and the Fae of Vale Woods."

She smiled gratefully and dismissed his words with a headshake. It might be a contradiction, but he'd earned both. Then, she invited him into the house. She had a feeling she might need a friend in there.

In the sitting room, Nan sat on the couch with a teacup in her hand. A tray at the end of the table held a teapot and beside it lay two cups, one empty, the other half-full and sitting directly in front of the mayor. Mayor Sean Belkin rested in the large floral sofa opposite her with a biscuit between his fingers. The husky, middle-aged gentleman placed the treat back on the plate and stood as she and Cameron entered. He wiped his hands on a napkin and lightly patted his black hair to ensure not a strand of it was out of place, then he extended a hand to Carissa. She returned the gesture. Glancing at her nan, she saw no look of concern. Maybe the mayor hadn't shared the news.

"Your gran is very hospitable," the mayor's jovial voice boomed in the small sitting room.

"I'll leave the lot of you to it." Nan rose. Thankfully, even at seventy years and being fully human, she was still as "fit as a fiddle"—as she liked to say. She made a quick exit to the kitchen, which Carissa knew full well was still within eavesdropping distance.

Cameron followed Carissa over to the sofa where they sat face to face with the mayor.

"You know why I'm here, Miss Shae, and I must begin by saying that I'm very sorry about all this terrible business with what happened at your apothecary shop today." Carissa nodded. The mayor continued, "You'll forgive me, but I have to ask this once, and then it will be done and never repeated by myself or any of my staff." He shared a look with Cameron. "Are you in any way responsible for the death of Miss Morgan?"

Carissa felt a sharp pain in her chest. It passed with a gulp. Collecting herself enough to answer, she gave a firm, "No."

"Good." The mayor took a generous bite of the biscuit and wiped his mouth with the napkin before moving on. "The sidhe guard wants nothing of our cooperation. They've made it clear they don't want our interference. The brownies, of course, have already come to us, but I'm afraid there's little we can do. This is not the first time we've been left out, and I daresay it won't be the last."

Carissa tensed. At least Mayor Belkin believed in her innocence. But, it didn't mean much if there was no way for him to help.

"I appreciate it, but I know the sidhe will sort it out." Carissa wanted to believe it was true as she said it. The sidhe were good at their work, despite their disagreeable qualities. And she was innocent, after all. She just hoped that was enough.

The mayor disregarded Cari's comment. "If you were a citizen of Vale, I would let the sidhe "sort it" as you say, but I won't let any Mossie go without my help in something like this, rest assured. I'm working on a deal with fae leaders for joint investigations in the future. Until then, I'm afraid the only help we can give you will have to be discreet." He dipped the last of his biscuit into his tea. The room fell silent except for the crunching as he chewed. The mayor's eyes slowly turned to Cam. The chewing grew slower and a curious look settled into his eyes. He squinted at Cam. "I think I've just had a brilliant idea," Mayor Belkin announced. Carissa braced herself. "Cameron here will deviate from his chauffeur duties to help. Being fae-touched as he is, he might be able to get close enough to find some things out."

"Oh, I don't think that's necessary—" Carissa began.

"Absolutely, sir," Cam said. "I'm happy to." He turned red and glanced between Cari and the mayor. She knew Cam meant well, but the sidhe didn't like humans interfering with their cases. There was a real possibility if she and Cam tried to investigate matters, it would only make things worse for both of them. Carissa frowned deeply, but Mayor Belkin didn't seem to notice.

"Perfect. It's settled." The mayor folded the napkin and placed it squarely on the plate. Standing, he stuck his hand out again, "My condolences on the loss of your customer. I do hope you'll feel free to contact me anytime or call on Mr. Larke if you should require our help while we investigate the matter."

She shook his hand, resigning herself to the circumstances.

Belkin took his hat in his hand, ventured a few steps toward the door and then turning back, he said, "Of course, your father may also wish to be involved in an investigation. If he'd like to work directly with my office, I hope that you'll contact me right away. We would like to be as helpful to the fae in this matter as we can." Carissa assured him that she would but had no illusions about why he was being so friendly. Her father may not have been the leader of all elves of Vale Wood, but he was influential in the Otherworld. His friendship wasn't needed but might prove beneficial for any mayor of Moss Hill.

Cameron gave her a smile. "See you later," he said. Then he followed Mayor Belkin out the door.

"Are you all right, love?" Nan came out of the kitchen.

"I honestly don't know," Cari replied.

"A little lunch in the garden might make you feel better."

Carissa placed the cups on the tray with the teapot and cleaned up the sitting room table. The whole time she thought about Cam's words about the poison in the vial. If she hadn't seen it herself, she never would have believed it. There was no possible accident, though her customers might end up losing confidence in her after this. No, this was deliberate. She just didn't understand how.

"If you'll pick some mint leaves for the tea," Nan continued, "we can sit out in the garden for lunch and you can tell me all about this business about a murder."

Carissa set the tray down by the sink. She could've hugged Nan, but her grandmother would've just complained about being kept from preparing the finger sandwiches she had strewn all over the counter.

Herbs and Homicide

"*Deep feelings are for treasured moments and poetry,*" Nan always said. Though she seemed to take things lightly, Nan also knew exactly how to ease Carissa's burdens. When Cari was feeling heavyhearted, even when she was a child and her parents went off on holiday and left her with her nan, she found solace in the garden. When she was school-aged, her mother wanted her to have a formal human education; her father, a taste of faerie culture. And so summers were spent in the Otherworld with the elves, and school years were spent in Moss Hill with Nan. It hadn't been easy to miss her parents for most of the year and then spend her summers missing her grandmother. Still, she'd adjusted, mostly because of the garden—both the one in her parents' home in the Otherworld, and the one she was stepping into now.

The sliding door opened to a world all its own. It was still the human realm, but the nature faeries never seemed to notice that either reality was separate. Carissa breathed in ocean and flowers. She had grown up with that scent. It lingered everywhere, even in Mount Vale. Another constant was the nature faeries.

Mossies were familiar with the diminutive, human-like creatures. Nature faeries, also called sprites, were said to bring about the seasons with their magic. Of course, Mossies knew it was the nature faeries' connection to living things of the earth that gave them the power to make plants thrive and bloom or wither and fail. As small as the flowers they lived in, they were missed by most humans, except the ones who were looking.

Walking among the bushes, Carissa watered the plants and tended to the hyacinth. The little garden faeries fluttered up to circle over her head. Two scrambled and fought for space on her shoulder, pushing and tumbling over each other so that neither of them could take a proper seat.

"Hey," she admonished gently, "there's plenty of room for both of you." The two faeries, whose names—Hiya and Cynthia—were inspired by the hyacinth they often hid in, stopped their tousle and sat. The cloud of little trooping faeries had also settled. They were now strewn lazily across the flower tops, looking happily at Carissa as she filled the hummingbird feeders with the sugar water mixture.

She didn't feel like talking, but the nature faeries didn't talk anyway. They could feel what she was feeling though, and with every movement and expression, they gave her silent comfort. They did this for her as a child; following her from this garden to the one in Vale, and even to her dorm in college. There, they'd found a place in the flowers by the dorm window and around the tall tree that stood watch over the courtyard, where Carissa spent nights studying for her degree in herbal medicine.

The garden faeries were part of the reason she was able to handle the inconstancies of her childhood. She was comforted, even now. But, no matter how calming the sprites were, Carissa could feel her eyes watering as she thought about the tragedy this morning.

Miss Morgan was an enigma. On the outside, she wasn't pleasant nor well-liked, but it had been her who'd found the missing nature faerie the month before. Carissa had always suspected she might be more than she seemed. She had an odd way of offering advice, usually in a condescending tone, but the knowledge was often useful and necessary for Carissa and other Mossies. Carissa knew at least a dozen people who, at one time or another, had benefitted from the brownie's suggestions. She'd even helped Carissa when she'd first set up the shop, somehow knowing what she'd need for which Mossie, fae or human.

The customers had come to trust Carissa, in part due to her taking Miss Morgan's advice. They might doubt her now if they believed the poisoning was an accident. If the sidhe thought she was responsible for a murder, that would be much more difficult to handle. Carissa had to fight the impulse to cry. If she really wanted to get justice for Miss Morgan and clear her own name, she had to find the culprit responsible for the brownie's death. But, if she interfered in any way with the sidhe's investigation, she'd be condemned and unable to help

Miss Morgan at all. And she wanted to help. The question was how.

Nan came out with tea and her delicious finger sandwiches, interrupting Carissa's thoughts. She placed the tray on the patio table. Carissa joined her under the shade of the extra-large umbrella. The kids of the neighborhood were off at school and neighbors at work, so all was quiet while they ate their lunch.

Nan waited, saying nothing about Carissa's morning until she was ready to tell it her herself. When she finally did, Hiya nearly fell off her shoulder. Cynthia had to catch him before he fell. Chaos probably would have flicked him in the ear for his drama, but the sprite didn't seem to be in the garden at the moment.

"Do you have any idea who might be responsible?" Nan asked.

Carissa clutched her locket and stared at the floor. "She wasn't the friendliest brownie, but as to wanting her dead…" She closed her eyes and put her hands on her face, wishing she could undo the whole day. There was no magic she knew that could make that wish come true. She let out a heavy breath. "I can't imagine anyone who'd really wish her harm."

"Did Maren see anything suspicious?"

"There was only Sal in the Otherworld with me, and there was a...human," she hesitated, she supposed he was human, "who was in the store—with Maren at the time—in the human world, but it was like he could see us. He came in after she'd already drunk the tonic, so I don't think he could've done anything to it."

"When was the tonic prepared?" Nan asked. She was so logical, rethinking the string of events aloud. Nan had a Holmesian quality about her and a calmness about this whole situation that was amazing. Carissa tried to oblige her.

"Yesterday around lunchtime. I wasn't hungry, and Maren ate lunch out with her boyfriend, so I stayed and finished today's orders."

"Her boyfriend?" Nan adjusted her glasses as if that would somehow clarify whether she'd heard Carissa correctly.

Carissa chuckled. Maren had thought she was breaking the news regarding her few dates with John, but she had returned to the shop after lunch with him just yesterday. She may have said it was just a casual meal at the time, but it's not like Cari didn't suspect it at all. Not that it bothered her. She'd meant what she'd said that morning. She explained John to Nan.

"Good for her," Nan said. "Though I'm not sure how I feel about real estate developers in Moss Hill."

"He's been doing wonders with the ruins at Fairfield, from what I've heard. But that's not relevant to the kind of important thing we were just talking about." She kept a light tone but was feeling more and more of an urgency to get back to the topic at hand.

"Murder."

"What?"

"You can't be afraid to call it what it is. You think Miss Morgan was murdered, and if that's the case, anything and everything could be relevant."

Carissa failed to see how John's job could be relevant to Miss Morgan's murder, but she digressed.

Hiya tugged gently at her ear and Carissa could hear Cynthia smacking his back in reprimand. She smiled at the pair, but her stomach was tied up in knots, so much so that she'd forgotten to set a little food aside for her friends. The rest of the faeries had plenty of food from the berries and herbs in the garden, requiring more aroma than food in their diets, but Cynth, and more specifically, Hiya, were always demanding special treatment. Carissa broke the tip of a sandwich into tiny crumbs and placed them on the edge of her plate. The two faeries raced for the food and ate heartily, like two bees sucking up nectar.

"So," Nan said, "Maren and John came back from lunch and then?"

"I left, and John must have left soon after because I saw his car going past me on Greenfield. Then, Maren tended the shop, and I came home early to help you set up at the library."

"How much later was it before John left?"

Carissa shrugged. "Not long. Why?"

Nan just looked at her.

"No, Nan, it's not him."

Nan held up her hands in defense. "I'm not saying it is."

"Really? Because it sounds like that's exactly what you're insinuating."

"I'm just keeping an open mind." She grabbed the sandwich again and bit. Carissa was floored at how nonchalantly she accused her assistant's boyfriend.

"Within reason," Cari said.

Nan appeared to relent by nodding. Then, she resumed her line of reasoning. "So, Maren was alone with the tonic from two until about five in the afternoon?"

"Nan," Carissa started, "if you're suggesting Maren..." she didn't have the heart to finish the sentence but diverted straight to "she's like family!" Hiya and Cynth stopped eating and stared back and forth between Nan and Carissa, mouths agape. Hiya absently lifted a bite of bread to his mouth while continuing his eyes-wide stare. Without looking, Cynth held his wrist down. This provoked Hiya, and the two were fighting again. Carissa pulled them apart as Nan answered.

"She's like family, of course. I'm not implying what you think. You weren't there, so you wouldn't know who came into the shop. You could ask Maren who stopped by yesterday afternoon and investigate from there."

Carissa thought about it. Then she realized that both Nan and Cameron were overthinking things. The sidhe hadn't even had a chance to look into the matter yet. Perhaps that was human nature—to fear things long before they happened. But there was no use in getting ahead of themselves. The fae had ways of investigating that exceeded human skill.

"Nan, this isn't *Sherlock Holmes*. The sidhe guard is going to handle it. I'll cooperate with them. There's no reason for me to do any digging, poking my nose where it doesn't belong."

"Love, that might be exactly what you need to do. You may think they'll search every nook and cranny until they've found the real culprit, but I'm telling you that someone designed this to make it look like it was you, and if you want to find out who that is, you're going to have to do it yourself."

She patted Carissa's hand and did what she always did when she wanted her words to sink deeply into Carissa's mind. She gathered the plates and cups onto the tray, gently swatted the faeries off the plates, and left Carissa alone to think.

Chapter 5

Suspicious Strangers

Nan and Carissa, dressed similarly to their Sunday best, arrived early to help with last-minute preparations for the event. Unbeknownst to them, the new head librarian, Mr. Greer, had not only done the last-minute décor himself but had added a few little touches that made it all the more delightful.

"Welcome, welcome!" he said to Nan, greeting them both with gusto. Hugs were exchanged before Nan and Carissa had a chance to take in the full sight.

The Moss Hill Library, thanks to Nan's efforts—and to the patronage of several pillars of the community—kept their shelves plentiful and in pristine condition. The bookcases ran in rows angled around the help desk. From this location, one had a full view of the floor. This included the twisting staircase and open layout of the second floor, which boasted several stacks of its own. The walls were painted a creamy off-white, and the floors were a faux wood porcelain tile, no expense spared. While there were computers near the doors, they faced the windows, away from the books and closer to the librarian's office. This made it all the easier to get lost in a book without the distraction of technology. Or so that was Nan's reasoning when she asked that it be designed that way.

The only carpeted area was the reading corner at the far right where a wide semicircle was often filled with wide-eyed youngsters for storytime. It also regularly held teen book clubs or the occasional Moss Hill Literary Society Meeting. Tonight, the reading corner held tables along the back walls piled with books for signing. Above the tables, a pink and white banner hung on the wall. It read: *Moss Hill Literary Society Presents: Tea and Roses.* True to the promise, tea and biscuits were available at the center help desk. As a surprise to the poetry group, two bouquets of roses stood on either side of the banner.

"Oh, they're lovely, Mr. Greer," Nan said.

"A contribution from our most devoted patrons," Mr. Greer responded. Carissa didn't need to guess who he meant. The Everly's charitable donations had increased the library's funding since Jane had joined the literary society. It was a welcome change.

Mr. Greer and Nan quickly joined in the conversation as other members of the society and the public arrived. Carissa scanned the room for Maren. No sign of her yet, but Cameron Larke stepped through the door by Mayor Belkin's side. Carissa turned around, suddenly interested in the Chocolate Hobnobs. She picked one up on a napkin and took a hearty taste.

"Cari, good to see you," she heard over her shoulder. She expected it to be Cameron's voice or that of the mayor. Instead, she was surprised to see John standing to her left. She wiped her fingers and nodded, caught in the middle of a bite. Maren, followed by a beautiful woman whom Carissa could only assume was John's college friend, joined them as Carissa finished her morsel.

"Cari," Maren said. "Surprise! I didn't think we'd be coming, but Estella loves poetry."

Herbs and Homicide

John jumped in. "I'd like you to meet my friend, Estella. Estella, this is Carissa Shae. She's the one I was telling you about, the one who runs the local apothecary shop."

The tall, slender brunette extended a hand.

After traveling by boat on a windy day, Carissa's hair would have been frizzed, thanks to her human side. But Estella was picture-perfect in a long chiffon dress that couldn't have just been taken out of a suitcase. Cari supposed it wasn't impossible for her to have ironed the dress and tended her hair before changing for tonight's event, but it was just plain irksome anyone could look that good in such a short time. Still, Carissa exchanged greetings and gave a polite smile to the woman.

"Pleasure to meet you," the woman said. "John and Maren have told me so much. I feel like I know you." She placed a delicate hand on John's elbow. Carissa raised an eyebrow. Later, she'd have to have a talk with Maren about being a bit more aware of this green-eyed beauty cozying up to John.

"Oh, that's very kind." Carissa wasn't sure kind was the right word as much as unnerving, considering that she knew absolutely nothing about Estella. Still, she didn't know what else to say. There was something about this friend of John's that seemed off.

Her fingers had been icy. There was something about her eyes that seemed older than she outwardly appeared. She had a strange vibe about her altogether. Carissa ignored it as best she could and asked her if she'd had a pleasant journey. Estella skipped right over the question.

"John and Maren have been telling me about the death in your shop today. What was that you said, John, a brownie or something passed away?"

Carissa shot Maren a glance, which Maren returned with a sheepish frown.

Carissa had to respond, so she said, "It was a brownie named Miss Morgan."

"Oh, that's terrible." Estella gasped too loudly. A few heads turned in their direction. Carissa slowly meandered away from the snack table.

"Yes, it was terrible. But the—" she recalled she was talking to a non-Mossie and left out the sidhe, "—the police will attend to it." Then, hoping not to gather any more eyes or ears from the growing crowd, she added, "I'd really rather not talk about it."

"What I don't understand is, aren't brownies supposed to be kind? I don't know much about faeries, though I read a little about them on the way here since John says they're a big part of Moss Hill. From what I read, brownies are house faeries. They live in people's homes and tidy up or care for the humans housing them. They're said to be pleasant to be around, but it sounds like this Miss Morgan was a nightmare."

Another sheepish look came from Maren. Carissa had to fight the inclination to shoot daggers with her eyes. She really hated the generalizations humans always made about the different fae. She knew she should drop the subject, yet she couldn't help but correct John's misinformed friend. She backed toward a bookshelf so as not to be heard.

"That's just a stereotype," she said. "Most brownies are nice, just like most people are nice. Brownies have a range of temperaments just like everybody else, human or fae."

"Aren't some fae evil, though?" Estella asked.

"The same could be said of some humans," Carissa countered.

Maren spoke up, "I think she means bogarts and goblins and things like that."

"The unseelie," Carissa lowered her voice. The last thing she needed was for someone to overhear her talking about the dark faeries. "That's the general term for fae who have taken a less-than-kind approach to their interactions with both humans and other faeries. There are specific terms for some types of faeries who choose that path. For example, a brownie who has chosen to be unseelie might be referred to as a 'bogart.'"

"Wouldn't have surprised me if Miss Morgan was a bogart." Carissa couldn't help but give Maren another jab with her eyes. "Well, she was mean." Maren doubled down on her response.

"She might not have been the friendliest person deal with, but she was by no means a bogart. If we ever had to deal with a real unseelie, we'd have a lot more than complaints and rudeness to deal with, you can be sure," Carissa said. She felt like she had to stick up for old Miss Morgan. Whatever she was when she was alive, Carissa felt some compassion for her now that she was dead.

"You don't have any unseelie on the island?" This was a strange question. It wasn't that people weren't naturally curious about whether any unseelie existed in Moss Hill if tourists believed in the fae at all. Rather, it was the way the woman asked. It wasn't the natural curiosity of a non-Mossie nor the fearful questioning of a Moss Hill newcomer. It sounded almost mocking, as if she were positive she already knew the answer and was just teasing with the question.

Carissa tightened her jaw. "I can gladly say no. Moss Hill has been undisturbed by all unseelie for the last two hundred years. The only dark fae I've ever heard of were in stories."

"Wonderful," Estella remarked flippantly. "I'm sure I'll sleep better knowing my stay here won't be interrupted by any hobgoblin or whatever Maren said. I'm not sure if I believe in all of that, but it sure does make an interesting story." She waved a hand. "No offense intended."

John turned the conversation to how the humans of Moss Hill had agreed to live together in peace in this secluded pocket of the world. His recall of events was a little off, citing it as if a U.N. treaty had been established between them. The reality was more like a slow building of trust and understanding. This was followed by an olive branch of proposed friendship by a Moss Hill mayor to a group of curious elves two centuries ago.

Astoria Wright

"Don't laugh, Estella," John said. "You really have to see and hear the strange things happening in Moss Hill to believe it. Once you do, it's fascinating!"

Carissa felt eyes on her from the townsfolk who may have overheard snippets of their conversation. She was unsure how many of them knew about today's occurrence. It was likely they'd all heard something. She was beginning to feel that she shouldn't have come, Nan's night of accomplishment or not.

The event began with the contributors to the poetry book taking their seats at the tables. Mr. Greer opened with some thanks and a short bio of the poets. Notably missing was Jane Everly, though her bio was read. This caused a twinge of sadness in Cari, as she realized Jane was likely home mourning this second loss in her family. The poets were invited to recite their personal favorites.

Mr. Greer began by presenting Nessa Shae, the editor of the anthology and author of the title poem, *Tea and Roses*. It was written by Nan as an introduction to the book as a whole.

Cari beamed as her grandmother walked to the podium and adjusted her glasses. Opening the book, she read. Her voice had a playful lightheartedness to it.

> "*The problem with prose is,*
> *It's not quite tea and roses.*
> *Song and rhyme.*
> *The beauty of verse is:*
> *The soul of it traverses*
> *All of time.*
> *So, savor in the reading.*
> *The poems now proceeding*
> *Are sublime.*"

Nan read a few more of her own, as did several other poets. Some were moving, some funny. The crowd responded with the intended emotions evoked by the passages. Everyone, that is, except for Estella, whom Carissa noticed held the slightest of smirks from the first poem to the last. The one that caught

46

Carissa's attention most was read aloud by someone stepping in for Jane.

> *"Maybe emotions are like tug of war,*
> *Pulled too far one way then the other.*
> *Struggling for center.*
> *When one side is winning, it's hard to let go,*
> *Or fight against.*
> *If it's perfectly balanced, it becomes a tightrope,*
> *And you know you're waiting for the fall.*
> *If we tie each end of the rope to something,*
> *Then it's stable, unmovable.*
> *The problem is,*
> *We put happiness and sadness in other people,*
> *Then, inevitably, they move,*
> *And it's tug of war all over again."*

Carissa didn't know Jane well, but the poem was touching. Its origin, she imagined, most of the Mossies in the room knew. Her heart went out to Jane.

Once the reading was done, the crowd mingled and the book signings began. Carissa would have let any conversation about today's events drop, except she heard Mayor Belkin speaking on that very topic to a group of concerned Mossies. Carissa glanced sideways at Estella, who didn't seem to notice the mayor as he bellowed his assurances. Yet, it was likely her insistence on discussing it earlier that had sparked the discussion now.

"No, no," the mayor assured, "there's nothing to fear. The guard has everything under control. We're doing everything we can to aid in the investigation."

Mayor Belkin spoke with a confident timbre. Cameron, to his right, seemed to be trying for the same decorum. When his eyes locked with Carissa's, the act dropped enough for her to see his discomfort. His gaze lowered and he shifted on his feet, but he couldn't break away from the crowd.

Carissa wondered whether she ought to take Nan's advice and do a little digging of her own. Given that the patrons of the library were already riled up by talk of Miss Morgan's murder, it couldn't arouse any more alarm to pull Maren aside and ask a few questions.

Cari did a quick sweep of the room with her eyes. The poets were still busy signing as patrons wandered over to the tables. John perused the poetry book while Estella was immersed in a conversation with one of the attendees. Carissa took this as a chance to ask Maren about the visitors in the apothecary shop. She slipped her arm into the crook of Maren's shoulder and tugged her away from the snacks.

"Hey! You almost made me spill my drink!" Maren complained. They were about three steps into a row of books, out of earshot of most other guests, but not so far away as to seem suspicious. Maren held the paper cup in one hand, shaking the other so that a few drops fell to the ground.

"Sorry," Carissa said. "Maren, can you tell me who came by the shop yesterday after I left?"

"Why?" Maren asked, still distracted by the cup, which she was now wiping with her hand.

Cari glanced around. From the limited few between the stacks, no one appeared to be eavesdropping, but one never knew with Mossies. A vague answer might be best. "It's important. I'll explain later."

Maren crinkled her nose, unconvinced. "Well, let's see. Mrs. Harbridge stopped by to pick up some soaps and lotions, things like that. We chatted a while, and the store was empty other than her at the time. Um...then there was a woman, she bought some of the essential oils and a book, what was it? Um, oh, that's right, it was the short guidebook you wrote with your father."

Carissa bit her tongue. *The Otherworld and Other Things to Know* wasn't really a guidebook, and it wasn't really co-authored with her dad. It was more like a list of the few things her father had told her over the years that she had to take notes on to remember. But, since opening the apothecary, she'd gotten a lot of curious customers who wanted to know more about the faerie world. Although most were Mossies, not all had as much interaction with the Otherworld as Cari had. She decided to share her knowledge with them in the guidebook.

Maren had moved on. "Then there was a group, definitely tourists. They were asking about the old Fairfield Castle and such. They bought some odds and ends, I can't remember. A few more locals, I don't know, Cari. I really can't remember more than that."

"Anyone who could have gone behind the counter?"

"No." Maren shook her head firmly. "Definitely not. I was back there most of the time, and when I wasn't, no one even went near the counter without my noticing."

"Well, anyone mysterious show up? Someone out of the norm?"

"No. I mean, the woman was a little strange, but not a criminal type."

"Strange how?"

"She just had an odd vibe—stared a bit too long, seemed overly self-confident, pompous maybe. Not exactly rude, but not nice, either." Carissa wondered if Maren realized she was describing Estella. Speaking of the devil, Estella had somehow managed to saunter right up to Cari without her noticing.

"Are you talking about suspects?" Estella apparently had also been listening to their conversation, because she interrupted with too much enthusiasm. "What about fae customers? Do you think one of them might have done it?"

Carissa took a step back and tried to compose herself. This woman was something else. Maren acted like she wasn't annoyed at all, but Carissa couldn't see how that was possible.

"We closed the shop in the Otherworld," Maren explained. "We only keep the store open in one world if there's only one of us there at a time. It's easier to manage that way. Ooh—" Maren turned to Carissa. "Actually, there were two more customers. Barnaby stopped by."

Maren must've noticed Carissa's raised eyebrow because she added, "He came from our world, not the Otherworld. He just stopped in because he saw Jane, she was the other customer. He wanted to give his condolences to her. Did you know that Alden died last year? I can't believe it. Pneumonia, what a shame. Do you remember him, Cari? He was in our grade. I think Cam may have been his only friend."

Carissa felt her heart drop. She knew Jane's brother was Alden Everly, but she finally connected the name to the person. Cari still couldn't picture the face. She barely remembered him from her school days. He had been homeschooled—the Everlys traveled often. His parents allowed him to join them in high school to "socialize," though he rarely ever spoke to anyone. He was the shy one who sat alone reading books, the one Cam was always pulling over to join him and his friends. Funny thing about Cam, he was always in everyone's business, but he made it his business to care about people, too.

As if on cue, Cam walked in their direction with a perturbed look on his face. He greeted everyone with a polite, half-hearted smile. Maren went in on him almost immediately for his "spreading gossip all over town." Cam didn't seem to mind. He pulled the knot on his tie loose, still dressed in his chauffeur uniform.

"Cari, I need to speak with you," he said softly.

Carissa couldn't ignore Cam's obvious distress. She didn't hesitate to excuse herself and walk with him toward the library entrance. "What's wrong?"

"The mayor talked to one of the sidhe guards. Another fae-touched Mossie introduced them. The guards don't want any help from humans, but they did share a piece of information for our police to investigate 'if you wish to sentence her as a human'—those were their words." He was rambling, and none of it made sense.

"Her? Who?" The knot in her stomach was beginning to match Cam's necktie.

"You. They traced the poison to your herbal tonic," he whispered. Her whole face flushed. She wasn't surprised by the discovery. In fact, she expected it. But the fact that they were ready to close the investigation with her as the culprit couldn't be right. The sidhe did not work hastily or make mistakes. At least, she was pinning her hopes on that stereotype.

Cam was still talking, but it took her a moment to catch his words. "Impossible. I know you couldn't have done it. I think someone's trying to frame you." He put a hand on hers, which she pulled back instinctively. Only after her knee-jerk reaction did she realize she was shaking. His failed attempt to console her deepened the frown on his face.

"I-I didn't do anything. The sidhe will see that." Carissa tried reasoning aloud, though shock made her own words sound like they were miles away and muffled.

"No, I don't think they will. The sidhe won't go out of their way to clear a half-fae, and the mayor's not willing to interfere in their investigation for 'the good of fae-human relations.' I'm afraid if we want to clear your name, we'll have to investigate this ourselves like the mayor suggested."

She stared at him, her grandmother's words coming back to her.

"Now, do you have any idea who might've done it?"

"Everly." Carissa shook her head, trying to rile herself out of her shock. She didn't know why she'd said that. She didn't really think Jane Everly was responsible, but it was an odd coincidence she was in the shop the day before Miss Morgan's death.

"Jane Everly was in the Seelie Tree yesterday. I think we should talk to Jane and find out why she was there."

Cam nodded.

Carissa found Nan and told her she'd be home later, to which Nan gave a look of concern. A little reassurance and Cari was off. She just wished she could assure herself nothing strange or terrifying was about to happen as she left the library with Cameron Larke to investigate a murder. As if anything could be stranger than that.

Chapter 6

Stranger & Stranger

The Everly home towered over the town on four acres of lush green grass at the top of White Oak Cliff. This was a neighborhood of luxury homes up the side of Mount Aisling. On the eastern mountain, pronounced "Ashling" by locals, wealthy Mossies enjoyed the sounds of seagulls and the feel of ocean mist from the privacy of their mansion estates. Though the only real castle was the abandoned Fairfield Castle at the base of Mount Vale, White Oak's most prestigious subdivision, the Mistletoe Estates, boasted the richest, most prominent homes in all of Moss Hill.

The Everly's driveway curved in a broad circle. Cam brought the car to a stop in front of a garage as if he were familiar with the path. They walked up steps guarded by unique raven statues on pillars, which felt a little creepy, if only because dusk was just beginning to set. A short old man opened the door, definitely human, but thin and wary.

"Fudge." Cam smiled and embraced him, seemingly against the older man's will, who stiffened in his grasp. "I'm so sorry to disturb you and the family, but we were wondering if we could speak with Jane."

The old man's face apparently couldn't hold a smile, though it did attempt one. He led them down a hallway past a wide spiral staircase to their right. The glossy wood floors and varied types of paintings on the wall gave Cari the feeling she was walking through an art gallery. Carissa couldn't recall enough of her junior high art classes to name the styles, but it seemed they'd included them all. The architecture of the home itself was a modern Tuscan mix, with arches and wooden beams everywhere. It was a gorgeous home, but Cari sensed the grief permeating every space of the cold corridor.

"Fudge has been with the family since Jane's parents were little," Cam whispered to Carissa. "He's sort of the family's everything—chef, chauffeur, butler. You might be wondering about the nickname. Jane's father says he used to make the best fudge in all of Moss Hill. He won competitions for it and everything."

"And his real name?" Carissa bet he didn't know. She was right. Cam turned that lovely shade of red. She hadn't deliberately whispered the last part loud enough for Fudge to hear it, but it may have bounced off the walls given the halls' acoustic effect. Cam grinned.

They both grew solemn as they turned the corner into a round sitting room. Here, the two found Jane Everly seated at a bay window, staring out at the ocean. She looked as if she'd been dressed to attend tonight's event at Moss Hill Library, her hair in an updo and her yellow, A-line summer dress ready to be seen. Cari wouldn't have been surprised if Jane dressed like that regularly given the elaborate décor of the home and the wealth associated with the Everly name.

Carissa noticed a woman in the corner of the room: an attractive, middle-aged woman in a sleek business suit with a laptop on her lap. She typed furiously. The pair must not have heard them right away because Jane's mother, or at least Carissa assumed it was her mother given the hair color and similarity in facial features, burst out with a frustrated sigh.

"I can't do this." The woman closed her computer. "Your father will have to take care of this. He can't just pretend it's not happening."

Cameron cleared his throat. Both women looked up. Jane languidly turned her head, but her eyes lit up and she bounded off the bench upon seeing her visitors. A genuine smile graced her lips as she enveloped Cam in an embrace.

Jane was pretty, by all standards. She was a dark-haired beauty with pale skin and eyes the hue of the ocean on a stormy day. They were shimmering now, with unshed tears that had not yet been blinked away.

"Jane, Mrs. Everly," Cam acknowledged each in turn, "I hope you don't mind us coming unexpectedly like this."

"Don't apologize, Cameron. We're always glad to see you," Mrs. Everly said. The words were kind, but the tone barely differed from its previous harshness. Her dark eyes bored right into Carissa as they studied her face. Carissa's lips bent just short of a smile.

Cam jumped in with introductions, "This is Cariss—"

"I know everyone in this town, even if we haven't met," Mrs. Everly said without taking her eyes off Cari.

Carissa's face flushed. Did she blame Cari for Miss Morgan's death? She thought the woman might go on a rant about her, but Mrs. Everly relented her stare and rose. "If you'll excuse me, I have a headache attributable to Miss Morgan, and she's not here to properly blame for it nor cure it, so I'll have to say goodnight." Despite her bitter tone, Mrs. Everly's voice wavered.

Everyone had a different way of grieving. Carissa supposed the woman's passive aggression toward the recently departed was just her way of mourning the loss. It still struck her as odd. Jane's grief, unlike her mother's, was evident in her puffy eyes and her downcast gaze. She made no response as her mother left the three of them alone.

Jane smiled awkwardly. She offered to call Fudge to fetch them tea or snacks, but they declined. Instead, Jane and Carissa moved to the sofa, and Cam took a chair opposite them.

"You probably don't remember me," Carissa said. "I'm—"

"Carissa Shae. I know. I went to the apothecary shop yesterday to see you, but you weren't there. I wonder how you knew, though, that I wanted to see you. I didn't actually dare to say anything to your assistant."

Carissa hadn't expected her to be so open. She thought Jane might be hesitant to admit to even being in the apothecary shop, but why would she have wanted to see her?

She waited for Jane to continue, but Cam immediately chimed in. "You wanted to see Cari? Why's that?"

Jane twisted her fingers until they settled into a clasped knot and remained motionless on her lap. "It was about something Miss Morgan said, before she..." Jane looked out the window.

"It's okay," Carissa coaxed her gently, "whatever it is, you can tell us."

Jane produced a nervous smile and pushed a strand of hair back onto her intricately braided bun.

"You were always kind to Alden when he was in school. He spoke of you both highly."

She was full of surprises, or maybe just polite. Cam might have been friends with the Everlys, but Carissa barely knew Alden and knew even less of Jane. At least Alden had been in Cari's year, though they'd shared only one or two odd classes together. Jane had been several years below them. Since school, Cari had seen Jane here and there around town, maybe even in one of Nan's poetry club meetings, but only recognized the young woman as belonging to her name upon seeing her now.

"What did Miss Morgan say?" Cam was ever-impatient, but this time Cari was almost appreciative. Whatever Jane wanted to say was obviously rattling her. The longer she sat in silence, the more an eerie feeling crept up Carissa's back. A shadow fell as the sun disappeared behind the hills.

"Miss Morgan wasn't a normal faerie," Jane said as if divulging a great secret. "She knew things no other fae knew. People misunderstood her, even I sometimes did. Denny was always her favorite. She tried to save him. Her magic didn't work like it was supposed to, so she investigated. She wouldn't give up."

Both Carissa and Cam inched closer to the edge of their seats.

"The day before she died, she said that the winds in Moss Hill were changing and she could no longer stay with us. She didn't tell us where she was going." The pain in the girl's face rippled to the surface and tears moistened her eyes. "She was family. We didn't want to lose her. I didn't know where to go or who to talk to. I thought you might be able to convince Miss Morgan to stay."

Droplets fell to Jane's cheeks. Cam patted his chest and pants' pockets. Carissa almost hissed at him, wondering what on earth he was doing, but he pulled out a handkerchief and handed it to Jane. He was too late, though. She pulled a lace one out of a hidden pocket in her dress and hadn't noticed his gesture.

"Jane, I don't think she would've listened to a fae any more than a human. My being half-fae wouldn't have helped," Carissa spoke gently, trying to reassure her that there was nothing she could've done.

"Oh, no, Cari, that isn't true! She always said you were the hope of Moss Hill. Miss Morgan thought better of you than probably anyone else in this town!" Jane's breathing hitched. "It doesn't matter now anyway. She's gone, and she'll never come back."

Jane cried more. Carissa sat, astounded. She had no idea Miss Morgan even thought positively of her. She'd been as grouchy to the apothecary as to anyone else. Cari's eyes lifted to Cam. The chauffeur looked miserable. He gave Carissa a look of impatience, and she shot one back to tell him they were not leaving Jane in distress. Awkwardly, she put a hand on Jane's shoulder to offer support. Finally, the young woman sniffled, and her breathing returned to normal.

"Sorry," she said. "I'm such a mess."

"No worries," Carissa said. "We understand. We're here for you if you need anything."

"Absolutely." Cam nodded.

"Do you know yet...?" Carissa hesitated to ask but felt a need to. "Do you know when the funeral will be?"

Jane shook her head. "There isn't going to be a funeral. Miss Morgan's sister is going to have her cremated. She went to Vale this afternoon to arrange everything." Her eyes threatened tears again.

Carissa looked at Cam. He still looked uneasy but didn't seem to be thinking what Cari was thinking. If they weren't having a funeral, what exactly was Jane's mother wanting her husband to arrange? She shrugged it off. The Everlys ran an international shipping company, Everly Exports. More recently, the title had changed to Everly Exports and Excursions, as the company expanded to offer a ferry service for tourists visiting Moss Hill and nearby areas. She could have been speaking of anything related to the business. Still, she'd make a mental note of that just in case.

"If you need anything at all, come by the shop," Carissa told Jane. "If I'm not there, Maren always knows where to find me."

Jane nodded and attempted another smile. They waited politely until she was in better condition, then excused themselves and left. The night air did little to relieve their tension.

"That was strange." Carissa couldn't help but say something as they walked down the steps to the driveway.

"What do you mean?"

"I don't know, I guess it was their grief. The whole thing felt sad and cold, like Jane and her mother were both mourning on their own."

"What's sad is that's normal. It's always like that in their house." Cam walked a few steps ahead, fumbling for his keys.

Carissa lagged behind, thinking about Alden. She was beginning to understand him better. Growing up in that house must have been hard for him. No wonder he'd been such a quiet person.

A rustling in the trees shook her out of her thoughts. Carissa glanced up and saw a black silhouette near the shrubbery on the side of the house.

"Who's that?" she whispered to Cam. He paused and turned around to look at her. She was already walking to the garden area past an unlocked gate. She saw a figure rush past as soon as the gate opened.

"Um, maybe we shouldn't," Cam's reply met the empty air. Carissa had already sprinted over the grass, her feet barely making contact. The figure dashed through the hedgerow effortlessly. She thought she'd lost it until she turned around the bend. She stopped and gasped. In the eerie moonlight, the man's upturned face was that of a skeleton.

"Hey! Give me a little warning next time—whoa!" Cam saw the deathlike figure at the end of the lane and skidded to a stop.

Carissa felt Cam's arm on her wrist pulling her back, but she didn't so much as look away as the mysterious stranger lowered his head to stare at them. As his eyes met hers, his face changed to that of a handsome man, near thirty in age. There was no mistaking his ice blue eyes and striking features. He was in the Seelie Tree this morning.

"Alden?" Cam said. His voice was shaking like a man who'd just seen a ghost, which, based on what they'd just witnessed, Carissa was certain they had.

Chapter 7

Dog of Death

Carissa pulled her hand away from Cam, who had only tightened his grasp upon recognizing his friend.

"Alden Everly?" Carissa's surprise highlighted her tone.

Alden smiled, a seeming friendliness that only made him appear more human. She hadn't seen Alden since high school, but the moment she realized who he was, the similarities became apparent. There was no mistaking him as anyone else.

"How?" Cam asked, standing close enough to Carissa that she could sense him shivering. The night air was cool, but not cold enough to make a person shake like that.

The specter that was Alden spoke. His speech began with the reverberating sound of multiple voices—or rather, one voice out of sync with a single reality. "I was the last to pass in the year," the voice coalesced into one. "Just at the winter solstice." Carissa couldn't recall but assumed that this was the way he'd sounded in life. It was calm and kind, a pleasant-sounding voice.

"So?" Cam's voice seemed to have risen an octave. For someone so proud of his fae heritage, he didn't seem to know much about the Otherworld.

Carissa explained, "He's the new ankou of Moss Hill."

"Ankou?" It took a moment for it to sink in before Cameron wailed, "Oh no, you're joking! The Grim Reaper?" He bent over sharply, clutching his side. "I think I'm going to be sick."

Carissa might have been scared except that she and Alden exchanged a glance that expressed both of their amusement at how poorly Cam was handling this. Carissa rubbed Cam's back at the base of his shoulder blades.

"Breathe slow," she said. He was hyperventilating. She breathed loudly for Cam's breathing to fall into rhythm with her own. "It's OK, breathe, just breathe. That's right, you're Okay." She coaxed him back to standing.

"Oh, boy. Okay, I'm okay." He stared at Alden. Cam's eyes were as big as the moon. "I don't believe it!" He kept shaking his head. He was still struggling to digest the revelation, but at least he was calming down.

"It's still me, Cameron."

Cam jumped at Alden's words. Maybe he wasn't quite calm enough yet. Alden's voice returned to normal. He even looked like his old self, though when he turned his head just so against the moonlight, there was that split-second in which she could see his skeleton. It came and passed quickly every time. It was easy to think it was some odd trick of the light.

"So, if you're the ankou," Carissa said, "you came to the apothecary shop to collect Miss Morgan's soul this morning. You knew she was going to die?"

"There are fae who can see the future, but I'm not one of them. I go where I'm called."

"Called?" Cam said. "By whom?"

The specter shook his head. "Not by a person. I can't explain it. I feel compelled to be in a place, and I'm there."

"So, why are you here now?"

"Relax, Cam. I'm not always on call. This is my home, remember?" He looked toward the light coming from an upstairs window. Carissa could see the slight transparency in his face, but even down to his bones, there was a deep sorrow that made her feel his human presence more keenly. That's what she realized she'd felt this morning. It wasn't a fae presence at all. It was that he did not belong in the human world anymore.

"I'm sorry this happened to you," Carissa said.

He turned to look at her. His eyes were blue, but the black center was hollower than a human's. The pain in his expression diminished, but the void in his eyes didn't.

"Sorry that I'm the ankou?" He gestured no. "I'm glad I am. Moss Hill just lost its greatest protector. It'll need us now more than ever."

"What do you mean?" Carissa asked.

"Us?" Cam asked.

Alden handed Cari a bag, a small burlap with drawstrings tightly tied. Carissa took it gingerly.

"What's in it?" Cam asked.

"The ability to see me and call on me when you need me," the ankou said. His head pulled back sharply, turning an ear toward the house. Now, Carissa could hear a sound, someone opening a door toward the back of the house.

Carissa had one last question to ask. "What do you mean Moss Hill just lost its greatest protector?"

Now, someone had clearly come out into the yard. They could hear the footsteps shuffling about on the pavement.

"Miss Morgan wasn't what she seemed," Alden said. "I'm sorry." He turned and disappeared against the backdrop of the garden hedges.

The footsteps grew closer. Cam and Carissa had no explicable reason to have come around to the side of the house. If they were caught, it would be difficult to come up with an excuse for their lingering on the Everly property.

"Let's go," Cameron urged. He led the way out the front gate and closed it, careful not to make a sound. They walked brusquely to the car.

They drove a while in silence. Cam appeared calmer, although far more focused on the road than was necessary. Carissa tried to process everything that had happened. Meeting the ankou was a new experience. She hadn't even known who the previous ones had been. It wasn't an unbreakable rule that the last person who'd died in a year would become the new Grim Reaper for a particular area, but it was the generally accepted norm if an ankou were retiring to the world beyond, he or she could pass the torch on to the last person who'd died by year's end. It must be a lonely occupation.

The ankou wasn't a member of the Otherworld and no longer a resident of the human one. His or her rightful place was in the world beyond either realm. Furthermore, an ankou was charged with the care of those who were destined to pass there, whether fae or human. This meant that they traveled between all worlds but were a part of none. It wasn't a role Carissa envied. She wondered if he'd actually volunteered for the responsibility. She voiced the thought out loud.

"He was like that," Cam confirmed. "I wouldn't doubt he'd have taken it upon himself to save Moss Hill. But what on earth could it need saving from?"

Carissa opened the bag Alden had given her.

"Wait a minute, shouldn't you do that another time? Like in the shop, or at least not while we're moving?"

"What do you think is going to happen, Cam? Think something's gonna jump out of it?"

"No," he said defensively. "Okay, fine. What's in it?"

She pulled the burlap back and peered inside, then rummaged through, taking stock. Now she knew what the mysterious stranger had done with the items he'd purchased earlier today.

"An herb mix, some mistletoe, and—" She pulled out a piece of paper and skimmed it.

"Well, what is it?"

"Instructions."

"For what?"

Carissa raised an eyebrow.

"Ooh no," he argued. "You can see him again if you want. I'll have no part of it, thank you."

"He was your friend!"

"In life!"

"Wow, nice to know your friendship has limits."

"Even in marriage, it's 'til death do you part."

"I'm sure your future wife will love hearing that."

Cam sighed. "All right. Fine. What do we have to do?" The car was turning slowly around Crescent Circle to her street.

"We'll figure it out tomorrow," Carissa said. Cam brought the car to her home and stopped. "Just meet me at the shop before closing."

"Fine. I'll be there." His grumpy tone was met with a smile from Carissa. She shut the door. Cameron stayed until she was up the steps and opening the door. Then she heard the car moving and turned to see it heading down the road. She smiled. No matter what his tone or argument, there really hadn't been a moment's doubt he would eventually come around. He was all talk about having no substance.

"Cari." She heard a whisper the moment she opened the door. Carissa spun left and right but saw no one. She noticed every single light downstairs was on, except the one in the sitting room where the voice had come from.

"Nan?" she asked.

"In here," came the reply. Carissa flipped on the light to see Nan standing near the sofa, staring out the window. She hadn't even expected her to be up. Nan turned and looked at her, wide-eyed.

"Nan, what's wrong?" Carissa hurried down the steps. Nan grabbed her hand as if to steady herself. The two sat sideways, facing each other on the floral cushions. When she calmed, Nan patted Carissa's hand and let go.

"There." She pointed out to the front yard, to the grass near where Cam's car had just been. "There was a big black dog in the road, howling like mad. I'd been watching it walk down the street for nearly half an hour. It ran off when you came home. Didn't you see it?"

"A dog?" Carissa's mouth hung open. This wasn't like Nessa Shae at all. As far as Carissa knew, her grandmother had never been afraid of anything in her life, least of all a dog

Nan shook her head. "Not a dog. The Black Dog of Death."

Carissa's face likely exuded skepticism. Nan responded with a smirk and an eye roll. It was a signature look Carissa shared, best used for showing frustration. "You've never heard of it, have you? Of course not. One hasn't visited Moss Hill since the day the last mayor died. He was a good man, God rest his soul."

Carissa gave in. The town was full of strange things. Why not this, too? "What is the Black Dog of Death?"

"No one knows for sure, not even the fae. There are several stories. Ghost, spirit, the ankou in another form. It could be anything."

Now Carissa was sure she was wrong. Why would Alden come here? And why in the form of a dog?

"Are you sure?" Carissa asked. "It might just have been a dog."

Nan shook her head vigorously. "There's no mistaking it. It was large and ferocious, darker than the darkest night, fur that shined like oil and eyes of flame. It was the Black Dog of Death, the barguest."

"But why would it come here? Did it try to attack?"

"No." A tingling came to the base of Carissa's neck. If it was the ankou, or in any way associated with Alden, it might have come because she was dying.

"You're not feeling ill, are you?" she asked. She put the back of her hand to Nan's forehead.

"No, Cari." Nan softly swatted her hand away. Her tone was gentler this time. "That's not what this fae means by coming here. I could tell by its eyes it did not come to kill or reap. It came to warn."

"To warn of what?"

"A person of great importance has died…or is going to. It will round up the dogs to lead a procession tonight. That's what the barguest does." Nan relaxed. Her hands came away from Carissa and shakily touched her own forehead. "That's all I know of it. I never entirely understood the fae; no human really does—not even a Mossie. Perhaps if you'd seen him, you could've understood more."

"I'm sorry I wasn't here."

"No, no, you misunderstand. I'm not blaming you. But you must tell your father. He might know more of what this means. I've given you the message, my part is done. I'm going to bed."

Cari leaned forward, placing her hands on Nan's shoulders to help her up.

"I'm all right, you can let go. I was a bit scared, that's all. I'm fine now." She patted Carissa's shoulder and made her way up the stairs.

Alone in the sitting room, Carissa switched the light off. Before turning to leave, she lifted the open curtain a bit higher and peered out into the night. The flickering light of the street lamp revealed nothing but empty yards and darkened homes. She believed the dog had been there. Yet, why had it come to warn them? If it signified the death of a person important to Moss Hill, Miss Morgan had not been that, she reasoned. Yet, Alden's words echoed in her ears: "Moss Hill has lost its greatest protector." Could Miss Morgan have really been that? If so, what exactly had she been protecting the town from? Carissa had an eerie feeling she would soon find out.

Chapter 8

Sidhe and Summons

The late night, or perhaps the shock of what they'd seen, took a toll on Carissa the next morning. She woke later than usual. Nan called for her to be ready for Sunday service. Father Quinn was a stickler for starting on time. With barely a half hour to get ready, she dressed in a floral summer dress and rushed downstairs.

"We'll have to take Chaos with us today," Nan said, stopping Carissa in her tracks.

"To the church?"

"That little nature faerie is all of a dither this morning, frightened as can be. It was all that howling last night. The barguest had his procession all right, all those dogs disturbing the neighborhood."

Had there been dogs howling last night? If so, Carissa hadn't heard it. She must have been exhausted. It was no wonder. She pictured Miss Morgan again. She had to physically rattle her head to shake the image away.

Carissa took a croissant from the counter and filled her mug with English breakfast tea. Nan lifted her cup, and Cari poured her seconds. Her grandmother went on, "She's disturbing all the other faeries and trembling out of her wits.

She can't be left alone, and I have the lit. society meeting today after church to discuss last night's sales, so I can't take care of her."

Last night's sales—Carissa hadn't even asked how they'd gone. She was so caught up with Alden and what had happened with the barguest, and now she was in a hurry this morning. She paused. "How did you do?"

Nan glowed. "Fifty-six copies sold. Not bad for one night. It's not a million dollars, but we've earned a few hundred for the library."

Carissa grinned and gave Nan a kiss on the forehead. "I'm happy for you."

Not being one to linger long on sappy moments, Nan changed the subject. "Now, go and get Chaos."

Carissa opened the sliding door and jogged down the steps, taking a sharp turn to the right. Hiya and Cynth flew straight to her, tugging at her clothes and buzzing in her ears. Hiya even pulled on her necklace, guiding her along the stepping stones to Chaos.

"Yes, yes, I know, I'm getting her, calm down."

She made her way to a hanging basket beside the kitchen window. Tucked inside was a flower pot with deep, rich soil. The drizzle of rain in the early morning darkened its coloring. The plant rooted in it was still only a bud. The deep red of the flower inside could only be seen in the lining where the green sepals folded over it. The bud drooped, bobbing slightly in the wind. Cari had been waiting for the bud to open, the chocolate cosmos was supposed to be as beautiful as it was rare, and she'd never seen one in person before it arrived with Chaos. Already the chocolate scent for which it was named wafted in the air and delighted her nose. But the plant didn't look well.

The chocolate cosmos wouldn't bloom until the end of summer, no matter how much Carissa and the nature faerie nurtured it. She leaned over the flower bud and squinted. Carissa understood taking time to adjust to new surroundings,

68

but it had been a few months since the arrival of both the flower and the little fae. This wilting was just too much.

"Chaos?" she called, scanning the soil. The faerie's skin blended with the soil, and her wings were a bright red when still. When moving, they shimmered and took on the coloring of whatever was nearby. Cari assumed she must be near the stem of the plant. She rarely wandered far from it when she was upset. Sure enough, there was the little faerie with her wings wrapped around her and her head down. Her hair was a tangled mess of light brown.

"Come on, Chaos," Carissa pleaded. "Won't you please stop sulking and go join the other sprites in the garden? They're really nice once you get to know them, and I just know they'll love you." She wanted to be patient, but time was flying.

"Poor thing. Have you been crying?" The little faerie nodded. Her face was wet. Carissa held a finger out, and Chaos took it. She pulled the nature faerie to her feet. Chaos grabbed the plant and stood there, hugging it. "You'll come with us today, all right? You'll be safe, I promise." Chaos nodded. Hiya and Cynth were steaming. Hiya turned a deep shade of red. "Stop it, both of you. It's not right to be jealous, and you know it. Now stop pouting and go have your breakfast. I want to see two happy trooping faeries before I get back today."

Cari realized taking Chaos also meant bringing along the flower. She removed it from its hanging basket and walked it through the house. Carissa spotted the burlap sack containing the items Alden had given her. For good measure, she scooped it up as well. She didn't anticipate calling the ankou today, but she'd rather have it just in case. Nan was already waiting out in the driveway, keys in hand.

"Chaos is one thing, but we can't take the chocolate cosmos," Cari said. "It'll look ridiculous, taking a potted flower into a church."

"We'll keep it in the car with the window open," Nan replied.

Nan's car was a two-door hybrid—fuel efficient—with a rack for Cari's bicycle in the back. It was small but airy, and with the fair weather and the windows open, the flower should be just fine.

Nan took the flower with Chaos clinging to it fearfully. Cari placed her bicycle onto the rack and secured it to the vehicle. This made them a little late, but Cari needed if she was going to work today. The Seelie Tree was closed on Sundays, though she generally spent some time after church restocking the shelves and taking inventory.

Carissa couldn't help but feel all eyes were on her before and after service started. With a hundred churchgoers, it was unlikely that was the case. Cari waved to Maren from her place in the choir, but, as usual, Maren was too nervous about her performance to notice. Chaos kept to her hiding place in Cari's purse, but she noted the sprite fluttering up between the seats to get a look at the pulpit. Once, she caught sight of the faerie swaying to the songs. Cari was glad Chaos was enjoying herself.

After service, rather than socializing with the congregation on their informal Sunday picnics, Carissa decided to head straight to the Seelie Tree. She couldn't take Mrs. Harbridge's concern or Mrs. Alcott's pity this morning. Maren saw no problem in staying, but supportive as she was, she insisted on going with Cari to work.

"You really don't have to, Maren. I'll be fine."

"No worries. I just have to change, and I'll leave right after." Maren took the choir robe off as they exited the church.

"Didn't John come with you?" Cari asked.

Maren frowned. "He said church wasn't really his thing, but I'll get him to join us." Her lips morphed to a half-hearted smile. Cari didn't ask whether he was with Estella. Despite her own dislike of John's old friend, Maren seemed to like her and trusted John. There was no need to put doubt in her mind. Maren and Carissa parted as the path turned.

Cari made her way to the car to get the chocolate cosmos and her bicycle. Chaos wouldn't have as much fun tucked away in her purse. She didn't seem to mind, though. She flew up onto Carissa's shoulder, fighting strands of auburn hair for a place to sit. Cari smiled. She'd never seen Chaos so carefree.

Watching the nature faerie, she caught a glimpse of the people who were making their way through the parking lot. Jane's family grabbed her attention. Among them, there was a woman she hadn't seen before. With the Everlys, it was possible this was anyone from a business associate to a visiting friend. Carissa vaguely recalled Mrs. Everly saying Miss Morgan's sister had come to Moss Hill, but this woman wasn't her. This was a human, near as Cari could tell, with long, black hair and much too tall to be a brownie.

As if she could sense Carissa's gaze, she turned. They locked eyes, and she didn't miss the slight glint behind the woman's stare. The stranger smiled as if she knew something. Or maybe it was Cari's paranoia. She looked back down to the faerie in the flower pot. Chaos didn't seem disturbed.

Scooping the plant up and unlatching the bicycle, she placed the flower in the basket and headed on her way. Maren was already there when Carissa arrived. The shop door was unlocked, and despite being closed, there appeared to be customers.

"Good morning," Sal called to her from where he was leaning against the back counter. He was there with a man and woman, all three huddled over the tablet console, talking to Maren. The woman spun around and Carissa recognized her green eyes, slender elven nose, and blazing red hair instantly.

"Hela?"

"Cari!" The elf maiden bounded over to her gracefully and wrapped her arms around her. "Oh—" Hela stopped mid-hug. She noticed the plant and pulled away, obviously not wanting to injure the young faerie. "Well, hello there," Hela said.

Chaos perked up, coming to the edge of the plant pot and peering over it with a smile. Carissa tried not to be bothered by the fact that Chaos never smiled like that at her, except when sweets were involved. Carissa understood being half-fae meant it would take longer for Chaos to connect with her the way she did with a full-blooded elf.

Hela giggled and held a finger out, which Chaos shook as if they were shaking hands. She couldn't get her to come out of the flower pot, however. There was a limit to Chaos's openness.

"What's wrong with her?" Hela's puzzled gaze followed Chaos as Carissa placed the flower down on the counter beside Maren. Chaos sat back down, hugging the plant again.

"She's been this way since she arrived in Moss Hill," Carissa said, but that was a whole other story she didn't want to get into. Instead, she asked, "What's brought you out here?"

"We came to see if you were all right." Sal stepped in.

"Of course I'm all right." She shrugged off the concern. She didn't want to be pitied or any attention to be drawn to her or the Seelie Tree. It was bad for business and for her own morale to be looked at with such concern.

By now the man had turned around. His long, blond hair, blue eyes, and bright smile were ones Carissa recognized as well as Hela's. "Fenigar, are you the elf she's marrying?"

Fen nodded, smiling. Hela's expression changed back to joy. She seemed to not have a care in the world. Her happiness might have been because of her upcoming wedding, but because Carissa knew her well, she understood that the cheerfulness was merely part of her nature.

Though Carissa was younger by much more than a century, full elves matured far slower. Odd as it might seem to those unfamiliar to the fae, Cari thought of Hela as a younger friend. She was the boisterous girl who loved dancing in the faerie circles and whom Carissa tutored, instructing her on human languages, specifically English, which was spoken in Moss Hill.

Carissa shook Fenigar's hand and took in the sight of them. The two elves blushed and locked arms with one another.

"I remember you playing that flute of yours at the faerie dances," Carissa said to Fen, glad to be on a happier topic.

She even spied Chaos's pleasant expression, with her hands on her chin and her elbows resting on the edge of the pot. "Never saw you dancing with any of the young elf maidens yourself. Glad to see that's changed. I'm happy for you both." Carissa needed the return to high spirits.

"But how are you, Cari?" Hela inquired.

Fenigar's expression was solemn now. "We heard about Miss Morgan—"

"—and we came at once to see you," Hela added. They made a great pair, already finishing each other's sentences.

"I'm fine. Nothing to worry about."

"But the dogs and all. Oh, you must be so frightened!" Hela said.

"Sal says there was a band of dogs going through the town and up into the Vale mountains last night." Maren seemed more curious than afraid, not a great attitude around unseelie. Unfortunately, she and the town were unprepared for any truly dark fae if ever one were to invade Moss Hill.

"'Twas the barguest," Sal said. He was speaking low as if The Black Dog of Death might hear and maul them on the spot.

"I know," Carissa said.

"You know?" Maren asked.

"It came by the house last night."

Hela gasped. Fen held her shoulders to console her. Chaos cried again, so Carissa walked over and put a hand on the plant pot, trying to calm her down.

"Oh, that is bad news. Very bad." Sal shook his head and tugged at his hair.

"Really, I'm fine. Nothing happened." Her grandmother's words came back to her. If Hela's family knew about the barguest, it was likely her father did, too, but she had to speak to him anyway. She had to find out what was going on.

"Sal, can you tell my parents I'll come around for dinner this evening?" She had to check. One never knew when the elf Dorian of Vale and his human wife, Kaley Shae, would be home.

"Dinner!" Hela burst out. "But that's another reason we've come. You must come for dinner with us tomorrow. It's our engagement party." She beamed.

"Of course, I'll come," Carissa said. Then she added, in as lighthearted a tone as possible, "Listen, don't tell anyone else about the barguest, OK? With any luck, anyone who heard them might just think some dogs were in a row. I don't want to scare anyone."

Maren and Sal both frowned. Hela and Fen had guilty looks etched on their faces.

Carissa closed her eyes and sighed. "You've already told someone, haven't you?"

"Barnaby may have come by—" Maren said.

"He'd have known the dogs were unnatural anyway!" Hela said.

"They were loud as can be," Fen added.

"All right, I understand. Just don't tell anyone about the dog being at my home." They nodded. She wasn't sure what good it did even asking. Keeping a secret in this town was impossible. She only hoped that was true for Miss Morgan's murderer.

"What do you think the barguest's appearance means?" Maren asked.

Loud knocking shook everyone to their shoes. There was no one at the door, and it was unlocked—on the human side anyway. Carissa and Sal glanced at each other, shaking off their fear. Of course, it had to be a fae. The shop wasn't open on the other side, the knocking was just a way of gaining their attention without having to switch between dimensions. Carissa shook her head. If it was Barnaby, she swore she'd blow her top.

She twisted her locket and immediately saw the sidhe guard, Varick, on the other side of the glass door. Hela and Fen evidently couldn't resist following her into the Otherworld. They appeared beside her and exchanged concerned glances upon seeing the sidhe. He stood straight and tall, his hands behind his back. Cari felt her insides seize up, her breath catching in her chest. This was terrible news, especially considering Cam's warning yesterday.

Her hands filled with light magic, which she used to unlock the door with a wave of her hand. She almost wanted to use the magic as a protective shield, but she dropped the energy back to an appropriate level once the door was unlocked.

The sidhe didn't move. Carissa frowned. He would make her walk all the way over to the door and open it for him when he could perfectly well do it himself? His bravado was astounding. She complied, her anger being replaced by annoyance. Rather than entering, he handed her a parchment. The fae were ones to stick to old culture, still using the untanned animal skin when they could have moved on to more modern methods of communication.

"I formally present you with a call from the Sidhe Council. You are hereby requested to attend an audience tomorrow at dusk in the Hall of the Daoine Maite." He clicked his heels and spun around, taking his leave. Cari could see the band of horses and other sidhe riders galloping through the street. In full uniform, swords glistening in their hilts, they stayed their horses, whose glittering bridles shone in the morning light. Varick bounded up on the saddle and took the reins. They rode off with the force of the wind. In either world, it was quite a sight.

"A call from the Sidhe Council! Cari, what do they want?" Hela had a fit, shaking so hard that Fen had to calm her down. Now Cari remembered why she'd spent less and less time around Hela in recent years.

"I'm sure it's nothing more than a normal part of the inquiry," Fen said. His quietude seemed a good contrast for Hela's dramatic flair. Cari didn't feel like smiling but tried for Hela's sake. She twisted the locket again, returning to the human world. They followed.

"What was it?" Maren asked. Cari handed her the parchment. Sal and Maren huddled over it, then looked up at her. The unspoken question was apparent on their faces.

"I have to go," Cari answered. "One can't turn down a summons from the sidhe."

"What about the dinner?" Hela asked.

"I can still make it." Carissa nearly laughed. She was enough of a fae to enjoy the contrast of a summons and a ceremony. "I'll just have to leave early." She realized that every fae at the dinner would be watching her, or more likely, bluntly asking her about Miss Morgan. That would be uncomfortable. But Hela's family were her father's oldest friends, so she really had no other choice.

"We can't get married with all of this going on, the death of a brownie, the arrival of a barguest. No, we'll have to postpone it." Hela looked up at Fenigar. He didn't seem as confident about the change in schedule.

"Nonsense. It'll be fine. Everything will work out far before your wedding, you'll see. There's nothing to worry about." Carissa tried to convince both them and herself of the truth of her statement.

"You have to come to the wedding, too. It'll be held at the end of the month. Say you will, won't you?"

"Of course, she'll come," Sal chimed in. "She'd never miss a thing like that."

Carissa smiled and nodded. Maren cleared her throat.

Hela took her hint and responded, "Oh, you too, Marnie, you absolutely must come." The elf didn't wait for an answer. "We've so many things to prepare. Take care, Cari." She waved and disappeared to the Otherworld, the other two fae following closely behind.

"Marnie? Do all fae have such a hard time remembering humans' names?" Maren was clearly annoyed, but Carissa couldn't help but laugh. It felt good, laughing, though one more terrible bit of news and she might have been bordering on hysteria.

"Maren, I'd rather not—"

The bell chimed, too late for Carissa to tell Maren to keep the news of the sidhe summons to herself. Maren's boyfriend and his friend, Estella, walked through the door.

"The Seelie Tree Apothecary," John said, "is the best link to the fae world in town."

"Hello, you two," Maren said. She walked to the side of the counter and hugged John as he approached.

Chaos shuddered and flew over to Carissa. She pulled at Carissa's sleeve. As Estella turned, Chaos flew behind Cari's back and out of sight.

"Hello, Carissa, how're things going today?"

"Fine," Carissa said. She could feel Chaos's nails digging into the back of her neck. She had to keep herself from wincing.

"This is a nice shop. Do you get a lot of business?" Estella asked. When she turned to scan the shop, Carissa put her hand to her neck and gently waved the faerie away. Chaos flew to avoid her hand and settled back down on her skin before Estella turned around. Carissa could still feel Chaos there, but at least she wasn't pinching this time.

"Enough," Carissa said. It was hard to act casual with a scared faerie clinging to her. "If you'll excuse me, I just have to check on something in the storeroom." Cari tried to exit gracefully, but it was an uncomfortable departure. She didn't want to turn around, what with Chaos hiding out behind her, so she took a few backward steps to the hallway, smiling as naturally as she could. Then she turned and ducked into the back room.

The frightened faerie glided into an open palm. Cari could feel Chaos shaking. "Calm down, little one. What's wrong?" The nature faerie looked toward the door.

"Something scared you out there. Was it the people?"

The faerie nodded.

"Was it Estella?"

Chaos just stared, fear fixed on her face.

"The woman, was it the woman?" Carissa clarified.

Now tears were springing to Chaos's eyes. She nodded slowly.

"Okay, it'll be okay, don't worry. We'll figure this out." Carissa placed Chaos on the desk, thinking. She wasn't sure how Estella figured into Miss Morgan's death, but Carissa was certain she did somehow.

Chapter 9

Accusations and Alibis

Carissa couldn't stay tucked away in the back room. If something was up with Estella, she had to find out what. She could hear the conversation through the thin walls. She knew if she didn't explicitly tell Maren to keep the news to herself, she'd end up telling John. She seemed like she was about to as the discussion veered back to what had happened in the shop yesterday.

"I didn't see it directly," Maren said. Carissa glanced at the door and back to Chaos. The faerie, as if reading her mind, tugged at her fingertips. Her eyes were pleading.

"I'll be right back," Carissa insisted. "You'll be fine in here. Just stay in the room. You'll be perfectly safe."

Chaos curled into a ball. She looked so frail and vulnerable, which did nothing to ease Carissa's guilt about leaving her, but if there really was some connection between Estella and Miss Morgan's death, she had to take the chance and find out more about this visitor. She closed and locked the back room door for added measure. All eyes were on her as she made her way out to the storefront.

"Everything okay?" Maren asked.

"Why wouldn't it be?" Carissa smiled again. She wasn't sure how convincing she appeared. She was so nervous she felt the tingle of elf-light emerging in her hands. She had to fight the impulse and breathe steadily to calm her fae instincts. "So, Estella, how do you like Moss Hill so far?" Carissa asked. She tried to be nonchalant as she walked to the front counter beside her assistant.

"It's perfect. In fact, I like it so much I might just decide to stay." Carissa turned to Maren, who smiled. Not the fake smile she gave when she was really annoyed. Cari could spot that one easy. This was real.

It was one thing not to be a jealous type, but here was an attractive woman who was far too friendly with Maren's boyfriend and she seemed downright happy at the thought of her living here permanently? It just didn't add up. Carissa took it as added evidence against Estella's case.

"Very different from your time in.... Sorry, where did you say you came here from?" Out of the corner of her eye, Carissa could see Maren raise an eyebrow at her line of questioning.

Estella smiled, though, and responded in a carefree manner. "I was at university in the U.S."

"Where in the U.S.?" Carissa asked.

"California. It's on the West Coast."

"Near Mexico, is it?"

One thing Carissa knew about Chaos was that the chocolate cosmos plant she had arrived with was native to Mexico. If Estella had been in the same area of the world at the same time as Chaos, that would be a connection worth investigating.

"I suppose so." Estella's expression turned quizzical, as did John's and Maren's. Everyone in the room was becoming a bit uncomfortable, Cari realized. It wasn't the questioning itself that was abnormal, but it seemed more like an inquisition the way Carissa was conducting it. She tried to make the conversation more natural.

"Mexico seems like it would be a good travel spot. I've always wanted to see new places," Cari said.

"You have?" Maren frowned.

Of course, Maren would catch Carissa in her half lie. Cari hated that her parents traveled so much. As a result, she was much more a homebody. Carissa tried not to give Maren a sharp eye but instead carried on in a friendly tone.

"Sure, have you been?" Cari asked. If she could just find a link between Chaos and Estella, that would be a start. Carissa caught the split-second where Estella's eyes moved to the chocolate cosmos plant resting on the counter. She recognized it, Carissa was sure.

"No," Estella said, but she seemed amused like she understood the reason for her asking. Of course, if she suspected Cari's intentions, she would deny anything that could arouse suspicion.

"Anyway," John looked back and forth between Cari and Estella, "I was thinking of showing her around Mount Vale today, especially the old castle."

Maren apparently picked up his change of topic and went along with it. "Estella's been wanting to see John's work on the ruins."

Carissa cocked her head to the side. The last she'd heard, John's renovation project had only completed about half of the mansion. She wasn't aware that any part of it was open to the public yet, as it was still under construction. "Isn't that a bit dangerous?"

Cari meant the hazards of the renovation work, but Maren took a different interpretation. "I warned them it was fae territory, but Estella has been learning a lot about them. She's fairly sure she knows enough of fae etiquette not to offend them."

Carissa studied Estella's face. "You've learned a lot about them in one night." Cari hoped Maren could see how impossible that seemed. All she did was glance at Carissa with eyes that said *what are you doing?*

"Well, I'll have John and Maren with me, so I'm sure they'll tell me anything I don't know." Estella's smile was devious. "It would be even better if you could come. I don't suppose you could take some time away from this place?"

Estella's answers were simple, and her demeanor so polite that if not for Chaos's reaction, Cari could have believed her suspicion was unfounded. Carissa felt inclined to take up the invitation, trap or not. But then she remembered the scared nature faerie locked away in the back room.

Her next concern was John and Maren. She bit the inside of her lip, debating. There was no reason Cari could think of for Estella to hurt them, but then, she hadn't been aware of any reason for her to harm Miss Morgan. But no, John and Maren were human. It was more likely she was using them than targeting either one. She might be using the outing to the castle to get to Mount Vale and its residents. The attraction was the closest one in Moss Hill to that area.

Carissa declined the invitation but shot Maren a warning glance. As friends go, Maren was generally oblivious to the little signs of distress a friend might usually pick up on. Today, though, perhaps due to Cari's odd behavior, she took notice.

"You guys go ahead, I'll catch up in a minute," Maren said. Cari glared at Estella's receding frame. She and John might not have seen her aggressive stare, but Maren certainly did. When they finally departed, Maren didn't hold back. "What was that about?"

"Didn't Estella seem odd to you?"

"She seemed odd? You're the one badgering her with questions like she's a...a—"

"A criminal?"

Maren glowered. Why was she defending her so vehemently? Cari switched tactics.

"Did you see how she looked right at John when she said she might stay in Moss Hill? She's sure been getting close to him in just a day, don't you think?"

Maren walked around the counter, touching bottles and packages in the first row. Carissa didn't have to look, they were all still facing forward from yesterday. Maren was just trying to occupy herself. "I'm not the jealous type," Maren said. Then she turned around to face Carissa. Realization lit her face. "Oh. My. Goodness," she said.

Carissa was about to nod, ready for her to agree, but Maren marched right back to the counter and leaned forward from the other side.

"You're jealous."

"What?" Carissa couldn't believe what she'd heard.

"I knew I should've asked you sooner about John. If you weren't over him, you could've told me instead of lying yesterday."

"What?" Cari repeated. "No, no, I didn't lie to you. That's not what this is about."

Maren placed her hands on her hips. "Then what is it about?"

Carissa couldn't come right out and say it, not with Maren in such a mood. She'd have to bring her around to the realization. But how? Carissa didn't know herself how Estella might have been involved in Miss Morgan's death. Thinking, she reasoned that if Miss Morgan wasn't who she appeared to be, maybe Estella wasn't either. Perhaps nothing was what it seemed. That would include Estella's arrival in Moss Hill.

"You said a woman came in the afternoon before Miss Morgan died," Cari started. "You didn't recognize her and thought she might be a tourist."

"What does that have to—"

"Could it have been Estella?"

"What? What are you on about?" At least Maren's hands were now resting gently on the counter.

"Maren, I'm serious. Could it have been Estella?"

"No, she didn't even arrive in Moss Hill until yesterday afternoon. I was with John when he picked her up from the marina."

"But if she just pretended to come in from the boat? What if she came on an earlier boat instead?"

"She did come on an earlier boat. There was a problem with the Everly tour line, and she had to take a standard boat out. She called John from the marina. That's how we had enough time to make it to the poetry reading."

"I mean an even earlier one. What if she came the day before?"

"Why would she do that?"

"To poison Miss Morgan!" Carissa's excited expression was met with puzzlement and sympathy.

Maren walked from her side of the counter over to Carissa. She grabbed Cari's shoulders. "Look, I know you're scared about the sidhe summons. John and I can come with you to the fae world if you want, for moral support. We're invited to Hela's matrimonials, anyway. Well, Marnie is." Her attempt to make light of the situation only made Cari feel worse.

She pushed Maren's arms away. "It's not nerves. I know Estella is somehow involved in Miss Morgan's death."

"And I know she wasn't here before we picked her up yesterday."

"Maybe you just don't remember. You said yourself you'd forgotten what the other woman looked like."

"Trust me, I'd know if Estella came into the shop the day before she arrived on the boat. A person would remember a thing like that." Maren sighed. "Can we drop this, please?

Maren left in a bit of a huff. For her part, Carissa steamed that her friend didn't seem to understand the gravity of the situation. Carissa's reputation, freedom, and possibly life were on the line. If Estella was innocent, so be it. But if she was guilty, time was running out.

With no one else in the shop, she let Chaos out of the back room. The nature faerie seemed at home as she zipped around. She spread enough fae magic to revitalize the fresh herbs and flowers, even through the freezers. She also helped herself to the aroma of the herbs. Cari filled the mortar with some choice flora. It was better for Chaos to eat in one place rather than her fluttering about the whole store.

Herbs and Homicide

Carissa contemplated her next move. Could she really concentrate on inventory today? Wasn't there something more productive Cari should be doing? She felt that she should take Nan's advice and do her own investigation. The problem was, Carissa didn't know how to go about conducting one. Should she follow Estella and John to Mount Vale?

She was just about to consider that as a viable option when the bell rang, announcing the arrival of Cameron Larke. Chaos stirred from her seat and flew to Cari's shoulder.

"You'll never guess what I found." Cam had made it across the store in a few giant steps. Once at the counter, Cam looked down to where Chaos waved a finger angrily at him. "What's wrong with her?"

"I think you startled her." The nature faerie gave one final stomp and then flew back down to the herbs. "Were you at service this morning?" Carissa noticed Cam was in a suit, which he always was as a chauffeur. Lately, that seemed to be every day of the week.

"That, and the mayor had me drop him off at the Everly's afterward."

"The Everly's?"

"Apparently, Everly Exports is in a bit of trouble, financially. They're working out a deal for a large contract with a foreign investor, which could increase commerce and tourism."

That might explain the arrangements Cari had heard Mrs. Everly speaking about the night of their visit. Could the strange woman have been the investor?

"Have you eaten yet?" Cam was leaning over the counter, trying to be nonchalant about asking her out to lunch. It was only lunch, why did he have to make it weird?

"Doesn't the mayor need you today?"

"No, the meeting's over. I've already dropped the mayor back home. Besides, he wanted me to look into the matter of, well, you know...so, technically, this is a working lunch." He stood up straight and walked alongside Carissa as they left the Seelie Tree. Chaos sped to catch up with them. She took a seat on Cari's shoulder, and the three of them wandered over to Gooseberry Bakery.

The scent of cheese and bread, pickles and pastries wafted through the air. It made Cari's stomach growl. Chaos zipped right to the glass and hovered with her finger tapping her cheek, seemingly giving serious thought to what she wanted to eat. The lunch rush was nearly over, so they were able to order relatively quickly.

"So, what did you find?" Carissa asked once they found a bright red booth by the window. Chaos sat on the edge of the table with her eyes narrowed on the waitress, tracing her every step until she brought their order.

"You remember what Denny said about Miss Morgan?"

Chaos ignored their conversation. Her eyes doubled in size as a fat, puffy croissant was placed on the table—all for her. She flew down and rubbed her hands together. Poised and ready to pounce, she was abruptly stopped by Carissa handing her a torn piece of her napkin. The sprite gave a grouchy glare and tucked it into her dress like a bib. Then she attacked. The pastry didn't stand a chance.

Concern graced Carissa's brow again, somewhat from Chaos's over-zealous indulgence, but mostly by what Cam had asked. "He said Miss Morrigan wasn't what she seemed."

"Not Miss Morgan, Miss Morrigan." He emphasized the "i" sound in her name and handed Carissa his phone.

Chaos stopped and glanced at the two of them. Then she held her belly, pointed at them, and laughed. When she was done, she gave a headshake and continued eating.

"Looks like Chaos knew that already," Cari commented, then glanced at the screen. "From the Moss Hill Fae Archives?"

"They've gone digital." He grinned. Then he turned to Chaos. "If you knew she was the Morrigan, why didn't you tell anyone?"

Chaos held both palms up in an I-don't-know gesture. Then she went back to her buttery delight.

Herbs and Homicide

Carissa didn't always understand Chaos, but it was fairly clear to her that the sprite had assumed they'd already known. But known what, exactly? Cari looked back at the screen.

"Read it aloud," Cam said between bites.

"*'The Morrigan is not a fae but is included in these pages as a part of the Otherworld lore nonetheless. No compendium would be complete without,*" she paused, *"without this druid high priestess.'*" She looked up at Cameron.

"Read on," he urged, taking a sip of his soda.

"*'Still mistaken to this day as a goddess, she is actually three druid priestesses consisting of Morrigan, Macha, and Babd, who are said to guard and protect their followers.'*"

"Moss Hill's greatest protector, remember? That's what Denny said. I think Miss Morgan is this Morrigan, one of the three druid priestesses who shared the name."

"That's a bit of a leap, isn't it? Despite what Alden said." Carissa didn't quite feel right calling him Denny the way Cam and Jane did. "It doesn't seem likely a druid priestess would pretend to be a brownie."

"Ah," Cam said, taking the phone back, "but if you scroll down, it says, *'The Morrigan changes in appearance from winter to spring, taking the form of a short old woman in winter months and a fair maiden in the summers.'*"

"It was summer—"

Cam held up a finger and kept reading.

"*She has the power to transform not only with the season, but at her whim.*" With that, Cameron clicked the phone off and grinned smugly, having proved his point.

Carissa had to admit he made a fair argument. "But if someone killed her...."

Cam's expression dropped as if the implications were only now occurring to him. "If it was an unseelie, do you think they killed Miss Morgan because she was protecting the town?"

"It makes sense. But if no one, including the fae, knew who Miss Morgan really was—"

"She was leaving." Cam interrupted. "Jane said she was leaving. Why would she do that? And why would anyone kill

87

her if they knew she was leaving anyway? It doesn't make any sense."

Cam was full of good points, but it wasn't enough.

"I think the only way we'll know for sure is to talk to Alden again," Carissa proposed.

Chapter 10

Spells and Specters

Back inside the Seelie Tree, Carissa pulled the burlap sack out from the counter. Summoning a specter, that was new. It felt even stranger to follow the directions written by the ankou himself. Cam gulped, visibly nervous, but he nodded anyway. Carissa unfolded the instruction sheet and began.

> "Five primrose ground with stone,
> A lock of hair, the ankou's own.
> Wild thyme, a pinch mixed in,
> Foxglove as a talisman.
> St. John's wort to protect,
> Ash bark, symbol of respect.
> Blended with a spark of light,
> Opens one to gifted sight.
> Add mistletoe to activate,
> Then speak, 'Show thee, ankou' and wait."

"Who knew Denny could rhyme?" Cam commented.

Carissa washed out the herbs Chaos had been snacking on and poured in the contents of the sack. She checked the instructions to make sure it was all there.

"Looks like it's all here," she said. She crushed the ingredients according to instructions, all except the mistletoe, which she assumed was used only when activating the spell.

"Did he really put a lock of his hair in there?" Cam asked.

"It's not like we're going to eat it, Cameron." She poured the necessary amount of the herb mix onto the counter, careful to save the rest if they should need to call on Alden again.

"We'll need a lighter or something for the spark," Cam said.

"My elf-light will work the same." It was probably what he intended, come to think of it. Carissa hovered her hand over the ingredients. Light generated at her fingertips. Cameron snuck the mistletoe in the middle, quickly pulling his hand away.

"Show thee, ankou," they said in unison. A small poof of smoke arose. Cam and Carissa both coughed. Nothing seemed to have happened.

"Maybe you should've used all of the mix." He took the list of ingredients out of her hands. They were both looking down at the items before they noticed Alden peering over Cam's shoulder.

"Oh, holy—why would you sneak up on a person like that!" Cam held a hand over his chest. "I think you gave me a heart attack!"

"Sorry," Alden said.

Carissa, who'd been startled too, did her best to not show it. "We think we know what you meant to tell us about Miss Morgan." She allowed Cameron to explain in more detail about what he'd found in the Moss Hill Fae Archives.

Alden nodded. "I only suspected it in the last month before I died. Miss Morgan confirmed it when she passed on."

"Confirmed it how? Do you mean she told you?" Cameron asked.

"There's more. I think I may know who killed her—or someone who was involved at least." Carissa described Estella, her strange behavior and Chaos's odd reaction to her.

"Where is Chaos now?" Cam asked.

"In the back room, resting. I'm sure she didn't get any sleep after the barguest showed up at our house last night."

"The barguest? It was at your house?" Cam gaped.

Carissa nodded, not wanting to get into it again. She turned to Alden. "You wouldn't happen to know anything about that, would you?"

"I know of the barguest. I've never met it. Though, Miss Morrigan was the most important person in Moss Hill, even if no one knew it. The barguest is not unexpected."

Cam lagged a bit behind. "So, you think it was Estella who killed her? But why?"

Carissa hadn't considered motive. All she knew was that something was off about the woman. She was lying about something.

Cam tried to make sense of it. "Do you think she could be lying about who she is? I mean, could she be fae?"

"Maybe. I get a strange feeling from her, but I can't place it."

"The unseelie have ways of cloaking their magic through trickery. Miss Morrigan was protecting the town specifically from the unseelie. If anyone had reason to kill her, it would be a dark fae," Alden explained.

A dark fae, a member of the unseelie, could that be why Carissa felt so strangely around Estella? Maybe Chaos could feel that dark magic, but there was more to it.

"Chaos acted like she knew Estella. And Estella recognized the chocolate cosmos Chaos is attached to, I know it. She was looking at it before she left. If Chaos knows her, maybe we can figure out who she really is."

"Or at least what kind of fae she is," Cam offered. "That's got to be helpful, especially now that Miss Morgan's gone. The Sidhe Council can only stop her if they know what kind of fae they're fighting."

"If Chaos recognized her, perhaps that would explain Estella's fear regarding Miss Morrigan," Alden said.

"What do you mean?" Carissa asked.

"Miss Morrigan was old, older than any normal human, and she experienced enough to know many fae. If this Estella has ever set foot in Moss Hill or come across Miss Morrigan in the past, it's possible she could've recognized her and thwarted any plan she may have had for Moss Hill," Alden informed.

"So, we identify her and then take the information to the Sidhe Council and wait for them to catch her. It's a plan, anyway," Cam said. He seemed relieved, perhaps too soon.

"If she saw or even suspects that Chaos recognized her, she might see you and her as a threat now," Alden said.

Carissa's eyes grew wide. She hadn't thought that Chaos was in any real danger, but if Estella could kill Miss Morgan so effortlessly, she might try for Chaos, too. There was only one course of action Carissa could think to take.

"Then we need Chaos to identify Estella and tell the Sidhe Council who she is before she has a chance to strike. She's been keeping up with appearances so far around the humans, but who knows when she'll change. She's with John now, but they're in the castle ruins on Mount Vale. I'm not sure if they went with a tour group. He could be in danger."

"Isn't Estella an old friend?" Cam asked. "What if he's unseelie too?"

Carissa waved off the question. "I've never felt him to be fae. Besides, many fae can shapeshift. If that's the case, she could've killed the real Estella and taken her form." Carissa's heart sank into her stomach. The thought this fae may have killed two people shocked and sickened her. Another part of her felt guilty for pushing Maren so hard to identify the customer from the day before. If she was a shapeshifter, there's no way Maren could have known that.

"We need to track her," Alden said.

Carissa nodded. "I'll look through the digital archive of the Moss Hill Faeries with Chaos. Thank you for that tip, Cam. You two can track Estella up Mount Vale."

"Why us? Alden's an ankou. I'm not exactly unkillable," Cam protested.

"Alden will be there with you. He can protect you," Carissa reassured.

"That's what I need, protection from a spirit! How's he going to help?"

Alden's face turned into that of a skeleton, causing Cam to jump backward. "I have my ways," Alden said. Then he returned his face to normal. "But I need a human to ground me. I can't stay in one plane of existence for long unless I'm attaching myself to a person."

"Great! That's just great. Now I have an ankou attaching itself to me. No offense."

"Always the team spirit." Alden smiled. Then he turned solemn. "Could you give me a minute with Cari? I'll join you outside."

Cam sighed. "I'll wait in the car."

Carissa titled her head and stared at Alden, wondering what he might want to say to her alone.

"I can't protect Cam, not entirely, and not if it's his time." Carissa's eyebrows knotted together. Why would he be saying this?

"I don't understand. Are you saying he's going to die?"

"No," Alden's response was hasty. "No, I'm not saying that. I told you, I can't see the future. I'm strong enough to handle a fae, and if it comes down to it, I can affect life forces enough to tip the balance in our favor in a fight, but if Cam does anything foolish, I can't promise I can save his life."

Carissa pressed her lips tightly. She wanted to prove her innocence, but not at Cam's expense. "Maybe he shouldn't go."

"It's not this outing that I'm worried about."

"What do you mean?"

"He puts on a show of not wanting to go into danger, but he's bound to rush headlong into it."

Sounded simple enough. Cari relaxed. "Despite all appearances, Cam's grown up a lot since we were kids. I don't think he'd do anything stupid."

A shadow passed over Alden's countenance. "Love makes one do stupid things," he said, leaving Carissa to stare at the shop windows, her mouth hanging open.

Chapter 11

Fear and Friendship

The Moss Hill Faerie Archives had no pictures of the fae, only descriptions. Still, Carissa read through the text, each entry at a time only to wait for Chaos to reject the title as the possible identity of the fae.

"There have to be over a hundred entries in here. We'll get nowhere like this. Can you tell me anything specific about Estella?" Carissa asked.

Chaos made hand gestures, first outlining a square, then moving like an orchestra conductor, waving little circles in the air. She put both arms out in front of her and made a giant ring with her hands horizontally, above the ground.

Carissa scrunched her face up and concentrated, trying to follow along. Finally, she gave up.

"I have no idea what any of that means." Chaos made fists and stomped her feet. "Well, don't get mad at me. No one would understand what that means." Chaos turned her back to Carissa. "Okay, tell you what, I'll keep reading from the list, and you just tell me if anything sounds familiar. You can have some of that lemon sherbet we have in the fridge while I read. Sound good?"

Chaos made a sour face.

"All right, we might have some cherry pops."

This seemed to appease the little faerie.

Carissa rose from the desk. Her eyes wandered to the Sidhe Council summons. She unfurled it and read it more thoroughly, now that her mind could process it more calmly.

Chaos waved around until Carissa's attention shifted back to her. She pointed at the door.

"Yes, popsicles, I know." Carissa walked over to the fridge in the front of the store where Miss Morgan had.... She focused on the ice cream instead of troubling memories. Carissa picked a cherry pop and unwrapped it, then took it to the counter where she found a paper plate to place it on.

As she did so, she saw Maren unlocking the front door and stepping inside. Cari felt a wave of relief. She seemed to be in good spirits, too, bounding in with a smile on her face. Carissa smiled back. Thank goodness Maren wasn't still sour about their argument. Cari was ready to agree to a mutual apology or even apologize for the entire argument; she was that happy to see Maren safe. Once she entered, though, it was clear she wasn't alone.

"What's this?" Carissa asked. Barnaby walked in behind Maren, taking his hat off as he cleared the doorway.

"Tell her what you told me, Barn," Maren demanded. The leprechaun, ever a helpful one, happily explained.

"Maren stopped in the haberdashery just now to talk to Mrs. Harbridge about Hela's upcoming wedding for advice on what would be a nice wedding present, and she was venting a bit about your argument—"

"Barnaby!" Maren interrupted, "just tell her the last part of what you were saying."

"So pushy," the leprechaun remarked. Maren glared, and he continued. "Well, I was in the shop two days ago talking with poor Miss Jane, and I saw the woman who came in that afternoon, the day before Miss Morgan's death." He paused and gulped. "She left when Jane arrived, and Jane seemed to know her. She was asking about something to do with her family's boating business. I heard her say something like,

'Don't worry, I'll have the contract drawn up as soon as possible.'"

Maren interrupted again. "A contract, see that?"

Cari squinted, perplexed. "See what? What does that mean?"

Maren shrugged. "I don't know. But it means something. I don't know really know Jane, but you do. I'd start by asking her who that woman is and what she's doing in Moss Hill." Maren looked like she'd just been awarded best friend of the year, never mind it was by a committee of exactly one witness. A contract could mean anything. She could be a client or an investor in Jane's parents' shipping and tourist service. Or, she could be a lawyer helping them with some business-related case. If Maren was implying it was a contract for something nefarious, Cari couldn't imagine it would involve the death of a house faerie. Still, Maren was trying to help, in her own way.

Carissa digressed. "You were right," she said, "Estella wasn't the one in the shop that day." It technically didn't prove Estella wasn't involved, but Cari wasn't going to go down that trail again. Besides, she wouldn't completely dismiss Maren's 'evidence.' She had seen the woman, or at least it could have been her, at the church on Sunday. "I apologize."

Maren's vindicated smile was replaced with joy. She waved off the apology. "Forget it, that's in the past. But, this woman, she might be the one responsible for Miss Morgan's death. If we can prove that, the Sidhe Council will have to drop any suspicion they have of you."

So, rather than just trying to prove Carissa wrong, she was genuinely trying to help. Carissa smiled, glad their friendship was stronger than an accusation against a friend of Maren's boyfriend.

Estella was still guilty. Nothing could change Carissa's mind about that. Maren didn't have to know that, though.

"Thank you for wanting to help, but I trust the Sidhe Council will figure this out," she lied. "I already tried investigating once, and it nearly cost our friendship. I think it's best to just let this go and let things play out as is." She hated lying, but Maren was wrong. She just couldn't see it. She'd only upset people and possibly get herself into trouble by going down the wrong track. It was best for her not to get involved.

"But if someone is framing you—" Maren argued.

"I'd rather not discuss it anymore," Carissa said in a stern voice. "Barn, if you have a minute, I'd like to discuss something with you...related to the ailment of one of your friends." She turned her attention to the leprechaun, who seemed confused by the request.

"Um, sure?" he replied.

Maren took the hint and sulked to the back room to put down her purse. Maren might be angry now, but better angry and safe than getting mixed up in any of this, especially when she wasn't thinking straight.

With her gone, Cari leaned over the counter and stared at the elf. He shrunk under her gaze.

"Wh-what's the matter?"

"You were friends with Miss Morgan," Cari accused.

"Who told you that?"

"Out with it, Barnaby."

"Fine, OK, so what if I was?"

"Did you know she was the Morrigan?"

He looked at her now. He appeared more shocked than afraid. "Who told you that?"

"Never mind. Did you know who Miss Morgan was?"

Barnaby gulped and retrieved the green cap from his head. He nodded. Carissa sighed.

"Do you have any idea who might have killed her?"

He opened his mouth, then closed it again. He looked at Cari suspiciously.

"It wasn't me," she said point blank, a little annoyed he could even think that.

"I know that!" Barnaby shot back. He leaned forward and up on his tiptoes, only the ends of his fingers touched the countertop. "There's a rumor it was an unseelie."

"What kind of unseelie?"

He shrugged but kept holding onto the counter. "Some of the fae say they've felt an unseelie presence the last few days. I don't know more than that."

Maren came back out. She walked right past them to the front of the store and flipped the open sign on. Barnaby let go and stood back at his regular height.

"That's all I know about the ailment. Hope I've been helpful." He winked. He made an awful liar.

Shortly after he left, Carissa told Maren she'd be in the back if she needed her. Maren didn't seem angry anymore, but she wasn't exactly in a great mood. Chaos was upset too when Carissa returned to the back room. That nature faerie pouted upon seeing the melting ice pop on the plate. Carissa set it down beside her.

"Sorry, but it'll still taste as good. Now, we've got a lot of work to do, so let's get to it, shall we?" Carissa scrolled through each faerie on the list. One by one, Chaos shook her head no, to the point Carissa wasn't sure she was still paying attention. They kept on until the end. None of the faeries on the Moss Hill Faerie Archives matched Estella's description. Carissa had no choice but to give up and tend to customers for the next few hours. It wasn't fair to make Maren tend the shop by herself, even if they weren't seeing eye to eye at the moment. Chaos stayed with Carissa, safely sitting atop her hair bun. Apparently, she was enjoying the view. Although she never left her perch, Carissa could feel her shifting weight and the faint sound of her giggling whenever she shifted between the Otherworld and the human realm.

By the time the afternoon rolled around, they were no closer to discovering Estella's identity. Cam and Alden had not found anything either.

"Nothing out of the ordinary," Cameron described the outing with John and Estella.

"The foreman gave them a guided tour," Alden added. "Estella never left the area."

"And after the tour?" Carissa asked.

Cam put a hand to the nape of his neck and rubbed. "About that...."

"They spotted Cam just before the end of the tour," Alden finished. "They invited him out to lunch."

"I'm really sorry," Cameron said, "but they're actually really nice people."

"It doesn't rule them out," Alden said, trying to pacify Carissa's rising anger.

"Well, of course she was nice! She wouldn't admit to being a murderer now, would she? She acted innocent because she knew you were watching." Carissa restocked shelves with more force than necessary. Chaos flew up and hovered in front of her face. The little faerie wrinkled her nose and crossed her arms. Carissa frowned, then offered her hand and settled her onto her shoulder. "I guess if I want this done right, I'll have to do it myself."

"That's not fair. What if Estella isn't pretending? What if she really is who she says she is?" Cameron suggested.

"You may have to consider that she's innocent. We could try investigating some other potential suspects," Alden said.

"The two of you can do what you want. I know there's something off about Estella. I'm willing to bet she's our culprit." It was becoming downright annoying how much her friends doubted her. Couldn't they see what she saw?

"We can keep tracking her if you feel that strongly about it," Cameron offered. Alden agreed.

"No," Carissa said. It wouldn't do any good for them to follow her when she had them both fooled. Alden made it clear that she was putting Cameron's life in danger as it was, and he'd proved to be lacking in tailing skills. It was risky for him to continue to be a part of this. "You've done enough for today." She knew her tone wasn't the nicest. Even Chaos tapped on her shoulder in reprimand.

Cam's eyes widened, and he blinked. His face reddened as if he'd been slapped. "I'm only trying to help you."

"Thank you, but I'll manage fine without your help from here on out."

Cameron opened his mouth to speak, then closed it again. He strode out, pushing the door aside.

Carissa locked it afterward. It was past closing time anyway. She turned around to see Alden in his skeletal form.

Chaos pulled at Carissa's hair. "Ow! Change back, you're frightening Chaos."

"Not until I make my point. Cameron was frightened of me and of what Estella might be, but he stuck with it anyway." He resumed his old persona. "He acted out of concern for you. What motivated you to treat him like that?"

Carissa didn't say anything but stormed to the back room and retrieved the sidhe summons. She handed it to him. He read it.

"*'Carissa Shae of Moss Hill is hereby summoned—*'"

"Not that part—read the bottom."

"*'Any and all parties aiding, abetting, or otherwise conspiring with the suspected, should she prove to be guilty, will be likewise questioned and open to charges of the same degree as befitting their involvement in the crime.*' But what does this have to do with Cameron?"

"If I'm found guilty of Miss Morgan's murder, Cameron, Maren, anyone helping me might come under the same fire as me. I can't risk that."

"But not me, because I'm the ankou." Alden's eyes closed and opened slowly as understanding washed over his pale face.

"No one has jurisdiction over you. You're the only one who can help me without being at risk yourself."

Alden handed her the parchment back. She took it, but he didn't let go. "You're wrong. The sidhe won't harm Cameron, Maren, or anyone else because we will find the real killer. All you needed is faith. Cam didn't fail you today. Your faith failed you."

Alden faded from view. Chaos hugged the crook of Carissa's neck. Her sympathy was the last straw. Now tears came unbidden to Carissa's eyes. She brushed them away.

"Come on, Chaos. Let's go."

Outside the shop, Carissa found her bicycle sitting on the pavement, tied to a meter. There was a zip tie around it that required her to go back in and grab a pair of scissors just to untangle it. That was Cam, even in his anger he cared enough to ensure that something of hers was safe and sound. It only compounded her guilt.

She used her cell phone to call her grandmother and inform her of her change in plans, then she took a right where the road curved at the top of the hill. Crescent Circle lay behind her. Ahead was Mount Vale, where her father might provide the answers she needed.

Chapter 12

The Fae Archives

Carissa used her elf-light to move with the wind. Her bicycle left a trail of luminescence behind it as it flew. Given the speed in which the wheels were turning, one might think the nature faerie would be scared, but Chaos seemed happy in the basket as the air rushed past her. The rolling green hills were replaced with the trees and boulders of Mount Vale. The ruins of Fairfield Castle cast a long shadow in the falling sun, and the trees became more ominous as the forest thickened.

It was too quiet in the woods for a summer afternoon, though it might have been Carissa's imagination that made it seem so. One could get lost if they didn't know the path, and there were plenty of fae scattered along the paths to lead a wandering human astray. Yet, Carissa had turned her locket to enter the Otherworld, and she knew the way well. She turned at the curves in the road, which would trick any normal human eyes.

She glided over what looked like rocky ground. It wasn't gravelly at all, but smooth and easy to traverse. In the Otherworld, she could see the fae homes where the trees formed archways and the hill that wasn't a hill became a set of stone stairs leading up to the fae village.

Carissa left her bike sitting against the wall from which the stairwell rose, and Chaos took her place on her shoulder again. Carissa smiled at how astounded the nature faerie seemed by the wondrous sight. It was like she'd never seen a faerie village before. Perhaps she hadn't. Carissa had no idea what her home had been like in Central America.

Chaos had come to her in a mysterious package two months prior with a message from a woman named Raven Corvus, telling her that there were "fae coming that you would rather not meet." Whomever Raven was, she had sent Chaos to help her identify these potential threats. Though why she sent her to Carissa and not the Sidhe Council was a mystery.

It was the sidhe who originally established this fae village thriving in a forest of redwoods. The homes were an unearthly blend of wood, stone, and glass so intricately shaped as to appear almost like an illusion that had grown out of the forest itself. The tops of the homes were covered in moss. The windows curved as if following the natural inclination of the wood they were made from, except instead of knots there was glass. At the right angle, they looked like cottages with wreaths on the doors, wooden steps, and even shutters. From other angles, there was just a door in a mound or an archway at the root of a redwood tree. In the human world, it probably looked like nothing more than a regular forest.

The village had no shops, but each person's home and garden were a place of potential trade. And each home did have a garden. The fae couldn't live without that.

At the top of the steps, Carissa was met with all types of forest fae. They greeted Cari as she passed.

"Good day, Cairn. Hello, Tierney. Afternoon, Avey—" and so it went down the well-worn path. Despite her friendly greetings and their replies, she saw the nervousness in their eyes, the shiftiness in their feet, and their urgency as they walked through town. There were fewer fae out than usual.

Deeper into the village, she eased somewhat upon seeing the smoke rising from chimneys and the greenery of the moss as the gardens thickened. Chaos happily swung her legs back and forth from her perch near Cari's neck. Her little feet hit Carissa's shoulder in a rhythmic beat.

"Will you stop that, please?" She bent her neck to look sideways at the sprite. Chaos only smiled and pointed ahead. About ten meters forward was the largest fae home, Hela's father, Rolin's palace, for lack of a better term.

Sal stood outside it with a basket in his hands filled to the brim with cloth, silverware, and other odds and ends. Since the fae couldn't pass another fae down the road without a hello, he fumbled with the objects in his hands and waved.

"How are you, Cari?" Sal called.

Carissa passed her parents' home to where Sal was standing. She came to a set of carefully twisted vines crafted into a gate, and Sal opened it to let her into his master's house. "That's all right, Sal. I'm not visiting Hela yet."

"Right, you're going to see your parents," Sal replied. Another fae passed—a gnome—and though he tipped his hat to them, he, too, shuffled down the road. Carissa chewed at the inside of her lip. Was it her? Were they also suspicious of her since the poisoning? Didn't they know her well enough to assume she'd never be capable of such a thing?

"It's Miss Morgan's sister, that's what's making them jittery and afraid." Sal looked at her with reassurance.

"What do you mean?"

"Miss Morgan's sister came early in the morning the other day to have an audience with the sidhe. They've not disclosed what it was about, but it doesn't stop the gossip and wondering. Especially since Miss Morgan passed not two hours after."

"She came to visit before Miss Morgan died?"

Sal leaned in. "Not just to visit. It was a matter of urgency." He set the basket down, taking a moment's rest. "That's what the talk is anyway. Who knows what the real matter is from what fae minds make of it?" He took a handkerchief out and dabbed his forehead.

Carissa realized he looked a little worn from all his work. She mentally tucked away the information about Miss Morgan's sister for future reference.

"How are preparations going?" she asked.

"Fine on our end. Fen's in a little trouble with the home crafting."

"Home crafting? Is he building a new home?"

"For him and Hela. Part of Rolin's condition for her marriage is that he should have a larger home for his most beloved daughter," Sal said.

Carissa laughed. "He'd better make it as big as the sidhe community."

"Bigger!" Sal joined in her mirth.

"I'd better get to my parents before they set out for another expedition."

"I told your father you were coming. He said he'll be happy to see you. They'll be leaving after Hela's nuptials." Sal reached down and heaved the basket up again.

"Where this time?"

"Something about an island, though he might change his mind. You never know with him."

"Thanks, Sal." Carissa turned back to the moss-covered mound, musing on her parents' next departure. That was Dorian of Mount Vale, ever an adventurer. Kaley Shae, his wife, and Carissa's mother, wasn't far behind in the carefree attitude that resulted in their nomadic lifestyle. They often reminded Carissa that were it not for her, they wouldn't keep a home to return to in the Vale Mountain woods. She doubted they would have one anywhere on earth, in either realm. Her grandmother would have never seen her daughter for visits or had a family left without a granddaughter to raise.

Yet, here she was. A lovely home and hearth came into view with smoke dancing across the top of a stout chimney, welcoming her. The fire made the whole entryway toasty, perhaps a bit too warm for summer. The furniture appeared as cozy as ever, and the plates were already set out for dinner.

"Hello?" Carissa called.

"Who is that?" Her mother's voice rang from the kitchen. A red-haired beauty appeared before her. "Why, my Carissa's come home!" That always annoyed her—the over-the-top greeting as if she never visited when they were the ones who were away for long stretches at a time.

"Yes, Ma, I'm here." Chaos, seeing the dinner plates, swooshed directly to the oval, tree trunk table. The sprite took a napkin and tucked it into the top of her dress and sat down.

"You've brought a hungry faerie, I see." Mother smiled. Carissa matched her mother's amused expression and explained a little about the new addition to the nature faeries in her garden. They'd missed Chaos's appearance in Moss Hill two months ago.

"She doesn't usually make herself quite at home as this," Carissa said. "She seems to be more comfortable around fae." Her mother might not actually be an elf, but this was a fae dwelling, by all standards. The hearth was the center of the home. The fireplace was a green flame in summer. Being faerie light rather than fire, it heated and cooled the residence to the perfect, constant temperature.

Above them, the wood of the roof ran in strands like waves. The indoor plants seemed to grow right into the walls here and there as decoration. The flowering vines adorned the lining of the windows. One, in the modest kitchen by the hanging teacups, swung open as Mother snapped the shutters and spoke to her father outside.

"Dori, come and see your daughter while I get dinner ready for all of us." Her father's face came into view at the window.

"Carissa, you've come at the best time." Her father's elf-light shown through the wall near the window, carving a line to form a portal. Carissa stepped through. She took her father's hand on the other side, and he pulled her to a set of stepping stones that led to a circular patio. Hundreds of nature faeries fluttered around her. A prism of light shone directly in front of her. It stretched from the sun to a fountain at the center of the circle. Her father ignored all the splendor and peered deep into the water.

Carissa looked as well. There was an image of a tree with fat branches all reaching upward, bare except for a canopy of green at the very top. It was as if the tree grew its roots to the sky.

"What is it?" Carissa asked.

"A dragon blood tree." The image vanished. "It's part of our next destination." The excitement in his eyes made them sparkle. She'd never seen him frown or worry.

"How long will you be gone?"

"Not long, four months or so." He walked back with her to the house. Carissa tried not to let her emotions show. It wouldn't rile him anyway. It was a surprise he noticed her demeanor at all, but he did, or else he wouldn't have tried to reassure her.

"You know this is my work. I'm a keeper of knowledge on the council. It's my responsibility to keep informed about fae around the world."

"Actually, that's why I came to you. Have you heard about Miss Morgan's death?"

He became thoughtful. It was as close to worry as Carissa had ever seen him, but nothing near what a human might show.

"The sidhe have informed us. The entire Seelie Council will gather after their interview with you."

"You know it wasn't me." She hated she had to say that aloud. Though she believed her parents would trust and support her, did they really know her after spending half her life a world away from her? Sometimes she felt they didn't understand her at all.

"Of course." Her father brushed off her concern as if it were nothing. He took a seat at the table, with mother and Chaos both listening in. If her father wasn't worried, at least her mother should have shown some sign of concern. Instead, she seemed utterly content as she put the last of the food onto the table.

"The whole fae council knows it couldn't be you, Cari," Mother said. "The matter is to find the person responsible, which is the sidhe's duty." Mother sat down and nonchalantly unfolded a napkin over her lap. Carissa wished she could be so convinced the sidhe would disregard the charges the same way they were doing.

"I think there may be another fae involved," Carissa speculated. "I met a woman yesterday who asked a lot of questions about the unseelie. Something felt wrong about her." She told them about Chaos's reaction to Estella and the Moss Hill Fae Archives.

"Yes, the Morrigan." Father nodded. "Her loss is a heavy blow to both Moss Hill and Mount Vale."

Carissa's eyes widened. "Did every fae know about Miss Morgan but me? For that matter, how many Mossies were aware of her existence?"

"I didn't know," Mother said. It seemed surprising the wife of the elf-historian—or knowledge keeper, as the fae referred to him—wouldn't know something so critical. Then again, according to Nan, Mother never really cared to know that much about Moss Hills history. She was more about the travel and excitement of the here and now.

"Some fae are old enough to remember her as the Morrigan."

"And what about her sister? Sal said she was in Vale this morning."

"Was she?" Father said. "Which one?"

"I'm not sure." Carissa realized neither Sal nor Jane had said. The Moss Hill Fae Archives had mentioned two. Cari wondered if one was likely to be more helpful than the other. She tried recalling their names, "Babd and Macha, I think that's what the archives had listed. Do you know them?" Carissa asked.

"Babd and Macha? I suppose those were names they went by. They went by many others, too. Humans know so little about the fae. I wouldn't doubt their lists are less than one-third of what we've recorded in our history."

"Would you mind if Chaos and I look through your records? I think she knows who Estella is, but she hasn't been able to tell me. She might recognize a description if we read it together."

"It'll be a long night working with a nature faerie." Her father smiled. Chaos didn't seem to notice his jab. "We should start straight away."

He walked to a cupboard near the fireplace and retrieved a hefty set of books.

Hours after dinner and several pieces of pie later, a stuffed nature faerie and two tired elves were nearly ready to give in. Carissa's mother had called it quits long beforehand and retired to bed. Chaos yawned and stretched her arms.

"There are almost a thousand entries here." Carissa waved her hands over the large leather-bound volumes laid out on the table. "It'll take hours to go through all of these. They're not even alphabetized. Most are just descriptions of historical events and dates. If we could at least search through them with some keywords." Carissa sometimes thought it an incredible shame the fae didn't embrace technology like the humans did. Her exasperated rant woke Chaos to full alertness.

"What would we search for?" Father asked.

"I don't know, female fae, unseelie, someone Miss Morgan might've recognized."

"Female unseelie who knew the druid priestess known as the Morrigan—it's worth a try." Her father closed his eyes, stood, and placed his hands out in front of him. The elf-light sparked from his fingertips.

The pages of the books flew. Some closed, others turned to specific pages, and a select few glowed with a bright hue. Carissa pushed down a tinge of envy in the pit of her stomach. Sometimes she felt inadequate to her fae side, given her father had left out a lot in her training on fae magic. At least he was helping her now. Chaos stood and hovered over each book, practically bouncing between them.

Father peered over the records too. "These are the female unseelie known to have been displaced from Moss Hill by the Morrigan," he said.

"There have to be dozens."

"'Dozens are not hundreds. We can get through these tonight."

"All right." Carissa cleared her throat. "Let's see, first one." She read the entry aloud. Chaos shook her head. Her father read the next one. Again, it was a miss. On they went like this until Chaos's eyes drooped heavily and her weary head shook "no" almost out of habit.

"How about this one?" Carissa read, "*The Leanansidhe*...." Chaos's eyes grew with each word. At the end of the description, she nodded and grabbed Carissa's hand. "It's okay, you're okay," Carissa soothed Chaos. She looked up at her father. "I think we've found her."

Chapter 13

Denial and Danger

Carissa moaned at the sound of her phone alarm. It took her a moment to recall she was still at her parents' home. She had a longer trek to work today than she usually had. At least she'd woken up with plenty of time.

Carissa stretched out her arms and rose from the bed. She dragged her feet to the closet. Her old clothes may not gather dust in the Otherworld, nothing ever did here, but they'd definitely gone out of style. It didn't matter much. Most of Moss Hill was out of sync with the rest of the world's latest trends. She would change before Hela and Fen's engagement dinner anyway. She picked out a cute pink top and jeans.

"Chaos," she sang out, "time to wake up." She didn't look to see if the faerie had listened. Instead, she walked to the outdoor area where a stream of water was sectioned off behind an intricate wood-laced fence covered in flowers to serve as a private bathing area. Nature mixed with a little magic did what technology could do for the human world, and both were beautiful to Carissa. Yet, being here brought out her fae side. She relaxed into her otherworldly nature, singing as she bathed, dressed, and walked with a little more rhythm. Her senses were heightened, and she could hear the fluttering of birds and butterflies in the garden.

She ran and leaped over the partition and back down on the other side. Her fae nature allowed her to glide along the thin wood. She came to rest on a set of boulders where the water flowed from a meek waterfall into the pond that came to rest in the center circle of her parents' patio. Rather than facing the pond, she watched the trees sway in the gentle morning breeze and listened to their song. Footsteps approached.

"Thought I might find you here," Father said. Dressed and ready for the day, and apparently helping with the cooking, he draped a terrycloth kitchen towel over his shoulder and leaped to join her on the stone. "Still your favorite spot in the world?"

She smiled and linked her arm through the crook of his elbow. "Always." She rested her head on his shoulder. They didn't linger long.

"Breakfast is ready," her father said. Then he kissed her forehead, and the two clamored down to race along the path of pavers that led to the kitchen.

"Morning, Ma," Carissa said. She closed her eyes and inhaled the scent of fresh bread and berry jam.

Her father waved a plate under her nose. "Better take some before it's all gone."

She eagerly snatched the food on the table. Cari bit into the warm, buttery bread, fluffy and moist, and savored the taste.

"Where's Chaos?" Carissa asked between bites. She noticed the absence of the chiming sound and the quick fluttering light. If she were here, she'd be zig-zagging between the serving plates to share in the meal.

"Probably out with the other faeries in the garden." Mother scraped jam onto her bread without looking up.

"She's probably enjoying being with a larger community of sprites," Father remarked. He followed Carissa's concerned stare out the window. "She can stay with us today if you'd like."

Carissa bit the corner of her mouth. Chaos might panic if she realized Carissa had left without her. Given what had happened when Chaos had first come to Moss Hill, she was still adjusting to the new people and places around her. Then again, the sprite had seemed more extroverted around full-blooded fae. Wasn't it good that she was out and about with other faeries?

"All right, thanks. Please keep an eye on her, will you? She's still easily frightened."

"Of course we will," her mother assured her with a smile. Father nodded before wiping his mouth with the napkin and asking her about what she planned to do with the information they'd found last night.

That was a good question. She hadn't thought much past discovering Estella's true identity. Murder investigations weren't her job. "I suppose I'll present the information to the Sidhe Council as a possible lead."

Father and Mother exchanged a glance. "The sidhe aren't inclined to listen to a sprite."

"You'll need proof," Mother agreed.

Carissa cast a downward gaze at her empty plate. "What would you do?"

"Gather some," Father said. "Bring either evidence to convince the council or convince a person of importance to speak with you on your behalf. Either one would make the council listen."

"Be careful," Mother warned. "Make sure to choose someone that council will actually listen to. It can't be a human." For a moment, she thought her mother was going to tell her to not put herself at any risk. Cari wasn't surprised by the fact that neither one of her parental figures was going to caution her to stay out of harm's way.

Carissa thought about what they were advising. Proof, that would be hard. She couldn't think of anything in particular that she could use to show that Estella was the Leanansidhe.

It wasn't like she could trick Estella into going with her to the Sidhe Council and revealing her identity. As for a person, Varick was unlikely to listen, and she couldn't think of anyone whom the sidhe would respect. Unless....

"There might be someone." Carissa pondered a while, then looked up. "But what about you?" she asked her father. "You're respected on the council. You believe Chaos is on to something. Do you think the sidhe would listen to you?"

Her father thought long and hard. "One never knows with the sidhe, but possibly. I would be happy to go with you, either way." It was a good backup plan.

Carissa rose and hugged her parents goodbye. She glanced sideways through the window. No sign of Chaos in the garden. She hoped the sprite would be all right.

Stepping out onto the path, she had the strange sensation she was being watched. Just out the door, she thought she saw a shadow move around the side of the house. Who would be lurking and scurry off instead of greeting a fellow fae?

"Hello?" Carissa managed to squeak out. Every hair on her head stood. She tiptoed over to the end of the wall. Taking a deep breath, she turned around the corner. There was nothing there but vines and flowers.

"What are we looking at?" a voice came from over her shoulder.

Carissa gasped. "Sal! Goodness, you scared me!"

"Sorry." The elfkin bit into a juicy red apple. He offered her one from a bundle hooked around his arm. She passed.

"What are you doing here?"

"Picking apples." By his expression, he must have thought his appearance was self-explanatory.

Carissa recomposed herself and started walking. Sal followed. "How are things going for the party?" Carissa asked.

He cocked his head to the side. "The party? Oh, yes, wonderfully! We're all set." He took another bite of the apple. Something about him seemed off, but Carissa waved it off as nerves. He was probably overwhelmed with all the arrangements and planning Hela had probably dumped onto his shoulders in the last few days. If fae were impatient as rushing water, Hela was a tidal wave.

"Any luck with your investigation into Miss Morgan's death? I mean, I assume you're looking into it yourself."

Carissa bit the inside of her cheek. Intuition was telling her not to say anything. She'd always listened to her instincts before. She wasn't going to stop now. But this was a nagging feeling, altogether different from the strong need to protect her friends that she'd felt with Maren and Cam. Why? Sal was just as close a friend to her as they were.

"No," she lied.

"Well, that's too bad. We'll all be hoping for the sidhe to go easy on you—I mean, for the sidhe to find the real suspect, of course." He smiled and gave her a wave goodbye, parting as they came to Hela's residence.

Carissa nodded and gave a polite smile. Confusion crossed her features and stopped her as she watched his retreating frame. Never had she felt so disturbed by his presence. For one incredulous moment, she allowed for the possibility that Sal was involved in Miss Morgan's death. He had passed her by for a moment, walking up to the counter. He had all the time in the world to place any kind of poison into the vial as she lay on the floor. No, Carissa had known Sal all her life. He would never do a thing like that. Aside from having no reason to harm Miss Morgan, it went against every aspect of his nature. There was no scenario is this world or the other in which Sal's guilt made sense.

But, the jarring feeling she'd gotten from him this morning had made it impossible to ask Sal about Miss Morgan's sister. She was someone the council would have to believe. Now, Carissa would have to find someone else who might know where she was staying.

Cari hastened down the steps and placed the book securely into the basket of her bicycle. She took her phone out of her pocket and pressed on Cam's number. Out in the woods, she needed a little magic to amplify the signal from the nearest cell tower. The light in her fingertips encased the phone and crackled in mini-sparks. The phone worked, but futilely. It rang with no response.

She shouldn't be surprised. She'd really hurt his feelings yesterday. She knew that now. She tried to push down the guilt rising in her gut as she grabbed her bicycle and started the long voyage back to Moss Hill. She'd try again later. He couldn't stay mad at her forever.

About fifteen minutes later, Cari turned the corner past the fresh, sweet scent of Gooseberry Bakery. The strength of the fragrance was muted, however, and seeing Barnaby wave from inside the haberdashery reminded her she was still in the Otherworld. Carissa hopped off the bicycle and began to turn her locket. She hesitated. Since she hadn't learned the whereabouts of Miss Morgan's sister from Sal, Barnaby might know instead. She fastened her bicycle and walked across the street to the leprechaun's store.

The place was stocked much differently than the haberdashery. In the basins by the front were stacks of needles and threads. On the racks hung cloth of all varieties. The ready-made clothes were neatly folded and stacked behind the store's back counter. Shoes and jewelry sat atop round tables that lined the store. In the human world, the basins held ties and tie clips, and the racks held suit jackets and other clothes. Here, Barnaby's creations were all made to order.

"Good morning," Barnaby greeted. "Well, this is a surprise. What brings you to my shop, Cari? Looking for a dress for Hela's party?"

Come to think of it, she probably did need a dress for Hela's engagement dinner. But that wasn't what she'd come to ask. Her concern was much more urgent than finding eveningwear.

"I came to ask about Miss Morgan's sister."

"Oh." The leprechaun shifted on his feet and pressed his hands together in a nervous knot. "I was afraid it was something like that."

"Why afraid?" Carissa recalled the tension in Mount Vale that seemed to be felt by all except her parents. She wondered if Miss Morgan's sister was someone to place hope in, or someone to be feared.

"I don't want to get mixed up in all this murder and such." He took his hat off. "Can't you just leave it, Carissa?" He must be out of sorts. He never used her full name or left things alone without any curiosity. He hadn't even asked about the book in her hands.

Carissa softened her tone. "I would leave it if I could. But if I don't do something, I might be blamed for what happened to Miss Morgan."

"Blamed! You? No." He waved his hands like two stop signs. "No, no, they couldn't do that. No one in their right mind would blame you for a thing like that."

"They already are. Now, help me, Barn. Tell me what you know about her sister. Is she staying in Vale or Moss Hill?"

Barnaby's shoulders sagged. "I don't know. But it doesn't matter. She'll find you, you can bet on it. I've never met her, but Miss Morgan always said she was the strongest one in the family and the most headstrong. She won't leave this alone, I can tell you that much."

"Which sister is it?" Carissa asked. She recalled the names from the fae archives. "Is it Macha or Babd?"

Barnaby held his hands up. "I don't know. I haven't seen her, and I haven't asked. There's a reason they were known as the triple goddess and a reason why they separated across the earth. They're more powerful and unpredictable than any fae." He shuddered. "Anything that drew her here is not something I want anything to do with."

Carissa thanked Barnaby and left. Peace and quiet met Cari at the Seelie Tree Apothecary shop. She tried to relax during the hour of looking through orders and mixing herbs without distractions. Of course, she was worried. In the back of her mind, she wondered how Chaos was doing without her, puzzled about what Estella was up to, imagined what Miss Morgan's sister would be like, and hoped Maren would understand why Estella was guilty. She fretted that Cameron would be too stubborn to accept her apology. Even though several lines of thought carried her mind through the hour, she arrived again and again at the conclusions that Chaos was fine; Estella could only be trying desperately not to incriminate herself; Miss Morgan's sister would likely help Cari; Maren would understand when she discovered the truth; and Cameron, well, Cameron would forgive her. Wouldn't he? She tried his cell phone one more time.

"Hi, this is Cameron Larke. If you missed me, don't fret, just leave a message and you'll have the pleasure of hearing my voice when I call you back!" The *beep* rumbled in her ear.

"Um, hi, Cameron." Carissa wasn't sure what to say. "I'm sorry about yesterday, but we really need to talk. Uh, it's Carissa," she added hastily. "Call me back." She barely pressed the end button before Maren arrived. Time for apology number two, this one felt less warranted than the last.

"Hi, Maren."

"I'm glad you're here," Maren said. "I want to apologize. I understand you suspecting Estella wasn't personal against John, and I shouldn't have reacted like that."

Carissa was taken aback. "Oh." She nodded and cleared her throat. "That's okay. John's your boyfriend, I get it."

"Well, you're my friend and what you're going through is hard enough without the strain in our friendship. Let's just forget it happened, okay?"

So, she still wasn't going to admit Carissa's suspicion was justified. Carissa just had to accept she couldn't tell Maren everything until after the sidhe guard arrested Estella. She agreed to Maren's terms.

"Good," Maren said. She walked to the counter where Carissa stood. "Now that that's out of the way, I think I've found Miss Morgan's killer." Maren's eyes lit up as she pulled out her phone. There were pictures on it—a woman fitting the description of the lady Barnaby had talked about yesterday.

"Oh no, tell me you didn't stalk this woman," Carissa said.

"I didn't stalk her, I followed her down a shady alleyway at an ungodly hour. She was talking to a crow. A crow, Cari. Can you believe it? A real oddball, that one is. Either she's crazy, or she's in league with a weird fae, like the highfliers a few months ago, remember?"

Oh, Carissa remembered. She recalled another "oddball" had been seen talking to a crow on numerous occasions: Miss Morgan. It was strange, but only for that reason. Could this mysterious woman who had visited the shop be Miss Morgan's sister? If it was, it didn't change the fact that Estella was the real guilty party.

"Maren, I appreciate the information—really, I do. But promise me you won't do anything else so dangerous."

"I wasn't in any danger."

"You followed an old woman down a dark alley in the middle of the night!"

"Well, when you say it like that—"

"I'm saying it exactly how you said it!" The ridiculousness of Maren's logic was astounding. "Just promise me you won't do that again."

"All right, I won't. But it's weird, right? You could take that to the Sidhe Council tonight, right?"

Carissa nodded. "It's definitely something." Then, she thought of another crucial question. "Why were you out so late? It wasn't just to tail this woman, was it?"

Maren clenched her jaw the way she always did when she was holding back.

"Maren," Carissa said more sternly. "Was Estella with you?"

"Fine." Maren folded her arms and gave a cross face. "Estella left her sunglasses at the castle and wanted to go back and get them. But John and I dropped her off at the hotel when we saw Macara, so she really has nothing to do with this, all right?"

Forgot her sunglasses? That was an unlikely story. If Maren couldn't see she was being toyed with, she was only fooling herself. But, there was no need to rehash the same argument.

"All right." Carissa let it go.

Maren unfolded her arms and tried to ease back to normal conversation. "So, what are you going to wear to the engagement party?"

The conversation turned to lighter things, and the morning went like a usual business day. They agreed that they'd cut the day short at around 2:00 p.m. since both had to prepare for Hela's engagement. Carissa printed up a sign for the door and Maren announced as the day drew to a close that she'd be going shopping with "friends." No need to guess who that would be.

"What do you buy an elf for a wedding present anyway?" Maren asked. The chime of the bells told them a late customer had arrived just before the end of the day. Maren glanced at the clock before turning her head to the door. The dread on her face turned to regret, and she faced Carissa, mouthing the words "I'm sorry."

It was John and Estella. "I told them I'd meet them." Maren made something of an apology under her breath. Carissa smiled as if to tell her not to worry about it. She knew it was a delicate balance trying to maintain a friendship on both sides.

"You ladies ready to come shopping with us?" John asked.

"Oh, I'm not sure Carissa wants to." Maren turned to Cari. "Do you?" Her eyes were pleading. Carissa wasn't sure if that meant please don't come, or if you come, please don't accuse Estella of murder.

"You go ahead, I've got some work to finish here," Carissa said. She managed as calm a tone as possible. Maren visibly relaxed and gave a smile that radiated gratitude.

Estella, whether she was aware of Carissa's suspicions or not, walked up to the counter confidently. "I'm surprised you're still working, though I guess it's good to keep your mind off what's going on with the murder investigation. Just enjoy your time and ignore everything else, you know?"

Carissa tried very hard to keep a civil tongue. "I'm not really the type to ignore my problems, but it's not going to be my problem for long."

"Oh, have you found your suspect?" Estella inquired. Maren's hands came together. It was a nervous grip, but Carissa saw it out of the corner of her eye.

"Only the sidhe can really say anything for sure." Carissa left it at that.

Estella nodded, and the faintest smirk appeared on her face. "Best leave it to them."

"Actually, Maren and I think it might be—ow!" Maren elbowed John's gut.

"Let's forget about it," Maren snapped. "Time's flying, right? We should go."

"Right." Estella leaned over the counter, her eyes narrowing. "You really should be careful," she hissed. "If the real killer knows you're on to them, someone might get hurt. That would be so awful." Estella's thinned lips curved into a haunting smile. Her eyes darted back to the door and she changed her expression to one of playful warmth and rejoined their mutual friends.

Carissa was near panic. She locked the doors, both magically and mechanically, and took the herb bundle out. Her fingers fumbled, spilling some of the thyme.

"Shoot." She gathered it back up and finished the chant. "Show thee, ankou," she whispered.

The wait seemed like eons.

Chapter 14

Cameron Calling

"Slow down," Alden said. "You think Chaos and Cam are in danger?"

Carissa inhaled, taking in all her frustration and releasing enough of it out in one breath to make sense again. "I don't know. Maren might be as well."

"Estella made a direct threat?"

Carissa recalled the words as precisely as she could. Alden's solemn expression intensified.

"All right, I'll check on Cam. You get to your parents and check in on Chaos."

Carissa frowned.

"What?" Alden asked.

"Would you mind if we switched? I've been trying to reach Cam all morning. Even if Estella hasn't hurt him, I'm worried I might have."

Alden stared unnervingly at her and faded from sight. She assumed the slight tilt of his chin meant he agreed, though a more obvious response would have been appreciated.

She tried the phone one last time, simultaneously turning the sign on the apothecary door to *closed*. The answering machine message came on again.

"Cam, call me back. Estella's at the making threats stage. I really need to know you're okay." Then, because she imagined a hurt Cam deliberately not answering the phone, she snapped out, "Call me back," in a less than friendly voice. If he were hurt, she'd be downright hostile to Estella, but if he were all right, that anger would be directed toward him.

She slapped at the light switch, slammed the door, and stabbed the key into the lock. Only after it snapped with a click did she calm down a little. She turned around and closed her eyes. Calm and focus needed to re-center in her mind; there was no place for fear and anger right now. Squaring her shoulders, she prepared herself for the worst, grabbed her bicycle, and set off down the road.

She didn't know exactly where she was going. She'd try the mayor's office. If it weren't for Cam not answering, she'd travel to the Everly's. Miss Morgan's sister might be there since that was the closest thing to family the brownie—no, the priestess—had in Moss Hill. It didn't matter, though. She cycled the pedals, traveling as fast as inhumanly possible. What mattered was that Cameron was safe.

Near the end of four miles, her phone rang. She slowed and stopped near one of the lamp posts by the local post office. The caller info on the screen read *Cam*. A thumping in her chest made her feel as if her heart suddenly restarted, though she hadn't been aware it had ever stopped.

"Cam?"

"Yeah." One syllable. All that worry and he sounded…disinterested.

"Are you all right?"

"Yeah," he repeated. This time he sounded annoyed, which only served to anger Cari.

"Where have you been?" she shouted, loudly enough a flock of nearby pigeons took flight and a few bystanders turned their heads.

"Around." Seriously? She might save Estella the trouble and kill him herself.

Cari looked around. She was near Main Street. A few streets down was a restaurant where they could sit and talk. "Meet me at the Second Street Pub. Now." In ordinary circumstances, she didn't use her elf-magic among the people of Moss Hill. Sparks flew from the spokes of her wheels as she jettisoned through the streets.

The Second Street Pub was a generally friendly atmosphere. Although it had a bar, the booths and tables were filled with families and tourists. It was busy, but the layout was spacious enough to allow for private conversation. Nothing reverberated off the brick walls, and the tourists were all too fascinated by the paintings created by local artists that hung on the walls.

Cari made it to the pub before Cam. When he did arrive, he was in shambles. His hair was a mess, his collar undone, his uniform wrinkled. He trudged to the table she'd chosen near the back and sighed, as if deflating into the chair. Carissa wasn't sure if she should be angry or concerned. She waited for him to speak first, but he didn't even look at her.

She straightened and leaned toward the table. "Cam, I know I was harsh—"

"What am I?" Cam interrupted her.

"Excuse me?" Her tone leaned more toward confusion than annoyance. Cam sat upright with more zeal than she would have thought capable given his demeanor a second ago.

"Every part-human descendent of a Gwragedd Annwn becomes something amazing in their time. My father, the medical director of the town hospital, my grandfather, a judge. Alden's whole family with their million-dollar company. What am I? A chauffeur." He huffed and slumped in his chair.

This is what he'd been doing all day? Feeling sorry for himself? "What's gotten into you?" Carissa asked. It couldn't have been just what she said to him yesterday. This was something else entirely.

"It's just, I was always planning to do something, you know? Be something. I've just never known what."

"If I've in any way made you feel—"

"Oh yes, by all means, apologize if you've made anyone feel anything. You can't have that, can you? Running your shop, taking care of everyone in town, bridging two worlds, healing and making everyone feel better," his tone rose. The lunchtime crowd would have something new to talk about if he kept this up.

"Cam!" She tried to calm him.

"But heaven forbid if you should make them feel something or feel anything yourself." He crossed his arms on the tabletop and stared into her eyes. She broke the gaze. He snorted.

After a moment of silence, Carissa recovered her resolve and faced him again. "Cameron, this isn't you."

"Sometimes, I wish I weren't me."

This admission caused Carissa frown. Something was very wrong with Cam. The more he spoke, the more convinced she became Estella had done something to him. She stood.

"Come on, we're leaving." Cam followed her out of the pub.

"Where to?" he said carelessly when they reached the car.

She snatched the keys from him with her fae magic.

"Hey!"

He wasn't exactly drunk, but he was under some kind of influence, whether of the intoxication or incantation kind. There was no going to the Everly's now.

"I'll drive." She popped the trunk and he reluctantly helped her fit her bicycle inside. Cam sulked the whole way to Carissa's house. She hated cars, but at least not talking made for one less distraction.

When they finally arrived, Nan was in a huff, complaining about the nature faeries. "They're all upset. Do something to settle them down, will you? They've been in my hair, literally, for hours today."

"What now?" Carissa grumbled under her breath. Cam sat on the couch, and Nan looked at him sideways, immediately perceiving his foul mood as uncharacteristic.

Carissa hurried to the garden and puffed, "Hiya! Cynth! Get your little sulking selves out here, now." She knew exactly which faeries Nan was talking about. She didn't want to be mean, but she didn't have time for this.

The sprites reluctantly flew out, Cynth practically pushing Hiya in front of her, and came to a halt on the table under the umbrella. She stomped up to them on the patio.

"Well? What's all the fuss about?" Carissa demanded. She could never be entirely angry at the sprites, especially when directly in front of them, but she tried to keep the edge in her voice to show she meant business.

Hiya started gesturing, Cynth moving her head to show agreement. Then the two switched, and Hiya's more rapid nodding displayed his support. The two kept pointing over to the basket where the chocolate cosmos plant had been.

Because Hiya's and Cynth's gestures were simplistic compared to Chaos's—and because she knew them very well—she understood what they were trying to communicate. It was pure jealousy, and Carissa made it clear that there was no excuse for that.

"Chaos's life could be in danger at this very moment, and you're complaining because I'm spending time with her instead of you? Really, I expected more understanding from you than that." The sprites' faces turned red. Hiya argued, even taking to the air to make his point, but Cynth pulled him back. "At least Chaos is helping," Carissa said. "She's trying to help find the fae responsible for Miss Morgan's death. You could learn to care more about what's happening out there instead of only thinking about who's getting attention in this garden. Now, I hope you can understand why I need to leave to make sure she's safe. Or do you really think it's more important for me to stay here and tend to your egos than going to save Chaos's life?"

Hiya and Cynth both hung their heads. Carissa bent close so that her face was right next to theirs. She softened her tone. "Chaos is not more important to me than you are. I care for you all equally, but she needs me right now. If you were truly good friends to me, you'd try harder to be a true friend to her and understand that."

Carissa gently brought the tip of her finger to Cynth's eyes, where tears were beginning to fall. Cynth and Hiya both hugged her extended hand, and she lingered with them a moment. Then, she said goodbye and walked back to the house. What a day, and the hardest part of it hadn't yet begun.

Straightening out the two faeries was easy compared to curing whatever was bothering Cam, so she was surprised to find that Cam was already showing marked improvement when she came back inside. He sat in the kitchen with Nan, two cups of tea sitting out on the table in front of them.

He stood when he saw her. "Carissa, I'm really sorry for my behavior today. I don't know what came over me, but you were really hurtful yesterday and," his voice changed from apologetic to angry and then hitched in his throat, "you're right, though. I'm useless to everyone!"

He was practically crying.

"Drink your tea, dear." Nan patted his arm with one hand while gesturing to the chair with the other. Cam sat back down.

Carissa looked at Nan with unrestrained confusion. The older woman got up and pulled Carissa aside, whispering, "Well, the tea is working at any rate."

"What do you mean? What's happening with Cam?"

"I learned enough from your parents to know a spell when I see one. Your guy there is enchanted."

Carissa frowned, partly from the knowledge that Cam was under a curse, and somewhat at Nan's use of the phrase "your guy."

Her hands fisted. "I knew it. It's Estella—it has to be. She knew he was following her."

"Don't worry, love. He'll be all right in a while," Nan said.

"You think the tea is breaking it?"

"It ought to, it's a powerful mix of herbs. Should take care of any faerie spell."

"What was in it? We may need it again if Estella tries something like this with someone else. Or better yet, we should make a tonic of it in case she tries her magic on anyone else."

Nan took her hands and reminded her of the here and now. "I'll make a few packets of the herbal mix. You get dressed for Hela's party, and I'll have him set right as rain and ready to go with you by the time you come back downstairs."

"Go with me? Oh, no, he wasn't—"

Nan's look could curdle milk. There'd be no leaving Cam here for Nan to look after. If she wanted an eye kept on him tonight, it would have to be her own.

"All right," Carissa gave in, "I'll be back down soon as I can."

"You'd better be," Nan said.

Cam was in tears now with his head in his hands, looking a downright mess. Carissa stifled a chuckle and bounded up the steps, relieved he was at least getting the spell out of his system. Carissa might not have been able to find Miss Morgan's sister today, but this was further evidence of Estella's wrongdoing. Still, it wasn't proof unless she had some residual left of the spell. For that, she had to take Cam with her. Whatever Estella had done to him, Varick might be able to see some trace of it. The Sidhe Council would have to believe one of their own.

Upstairs, she finally had a moment to think of Hela's party. For a dress, she could only think of one that would suit this occasion. She unwrapped the green silk her mother had brought back two summers ago from a trip through Asia. It had been too fancy to wear to the poetry signing, but nothing was too elegant for a fae engagement. For the gift, Carissa already knew what she would give Hela. She'd crafted it years ago and put it aside. All it needed now was a little magical engraving. With the words etched into it, it was perfect.

Chapter 15

Enchanted Evening

Maren and John joined Carissa and Cameron on the drive to the Vale Woods. She had never used her locket to shift an entire vehicle full of passengers into the Otherworld before. There was a first time for everything. Of course, the car had to be parked far from the village entrance as the tree line thickened. They had to hike a short distance and then up the stairway before making it into the fae village. Thank goodness she'd been sensible enough to wear comfortable shoes. She should have warned Maren about that.

John helped her as she lifted the hem of her dress high enough to watch her step. With her heels, Maren would have to tread carefully. She didn't seem to mind, though.

"This'll be so much fun. I've never been to a fae engagement party before!" Maren said as they finally made it to the stone steps. Carissa didn't point out to Maren that she hadn't actually been to the faerie village at all before. Maren kept chatting away. "I hope the present I've brought will be okay. It's so hard to know what an elf couple wants. You think they'll like this, though, right?"

"Yes, absolutely!" No matter how many times Maren asked, Carissa replied with a smile. Yet, the corners of her lips fell downward as she looked at the path ahead. A tug of worry for Chaos and the Miss Morgan case kept pulling at her happiness for Hela and Fen. As long as Chaos was safe, family and friends were all accounted for. Nan would be fine in the house with all the charms and the nature faeries protecting her. In the fae realm, Estella dare not cause any overt trouble. As long as they stuck together, they should be fine. Cam, who seemed to have fully recovered his senses, took a while longer than the rest, ensuring the car was safely parked. He caught up with Cari at the top of the stairway.

"I didn't bring anything," Cam whispered.

"Don't worry, my gift will cover us both."

"Good." Cameron sighed. "What did you bring?"

Carissa patted the small gold purse in her hands. "You'll see." Turning onto the main road, from which Hela's home was already visible, a shadow caught her eye. She tensed. She and Cam both looked to the right. They recognized the figure and turned to each other.

"I'll go," Cari said.

"Something wrong?" John asked.

"Nope," Cameron's overly-casual voice probably wasn't as convincing. "She's just taking a second to, uh, tie her shoe." He re-worded. "No, nope, it's a sandal, can't be tying it, she's just, uh, fixing it, you know—pebbles and all. Let's keep going, shall we?" He ushered them forward and looked back at Carissa.

She pulled an amused lip sideways as she heard the conversation behind her. Cam wasn't a great liar, but then, that was a good thing in most circumstances. Carissa came to the edge of one of the houses and turned the corner. A skeletal face greeted her, though it shifted back to flesh and blood soon enough.

"Is she safe?" Carissa asked Alden. Relief washed over her when she saw the little faerie floating above the ankou's shoulder.

"She's fine," Alden said, "she's been with me all day. We've been investigating around here. Cari, there are shadows all around this place, especially Hela's home."

"Shadows?"

"A shadow of death. When a person is going to die or becomes intent on killing, shadow forms over such people. It usually varies, like wisps of smoke. A person's fate isn't set in stone. Only when a person's mind is set on a kill—or a death is set to take place—does the trail becomes stable and unchanging. Everywhere the person sets foot, the shadow is cast. There are trails like that all around Hela's home."

Carissa swallowed her fear. If Estella were in Vale Woods, she'd have to be focused and clear-headed. "Thanks, Alden. Can you keep Chaos with you? I'll see what I can find out at the dinner."

"Be careful," Alden said.

"I will," Carissa responded. Chaos looked at her with frightened eyes. "I'll be okay," Carissa assured her. She wished she could reassure herself.

She rejoined her party just in front of the home. Sal greeted them at the door, arms wide open, with an exuberant, "Welcome!" He walked them to the back garden where faerie lights magically hung in the air and the longest table Carissa had ever seen was set with fine dinnerware that made Maren question her purchase again.

"They'll love the champagne glasses," Cari whispered to her nervous friend, then she turned her attention to Sal. "You seem better than this morning. Looks like everything came together for tonight."

Sal looked a little puzzled. "Yes, oh yes, everything is set to the minutest detail." He shifted his eyes to a group of sprites that had begun fighting over one of the hovering lights. "Excuse me." He hurried over to them.

The garden faeries, for the most part, were flying about, intensifying the colors of the flowers and brightening the greenery of the grass. The porch filled with various fae. Maren and John had already made their way to Hela and Fenigar to congratulate them.

Cam approached with two cups. "What did Alden say?"

Carissa took the cup from Cam's hand. She tried to keep her expression neutral. "Chaos is safe. Estella could be anywhere. Keep sharp." She took a sip. The delicious elderberry flavor tingled her taste buds.

"Should we mingle?"

"Probably a good idea. Cam, it's a party."

"So?"

"So, try not to look like an undercover agent from a spy movie." Cam didn't exactly relax, but his expression did change to visibly annoyed.

"Wait, come here." She adjusted his tie and leaned toward him. In full honesty, she said, "I'm glad you're here." He smiled. "You're a good friend." The smile dissipated, not entirely, but enough for her to realize she'd hurt him again.

She pulled away, her own smile becoming an awkward biting of her lip. She had been trying to compliment him. Why did Cameron always have to make it weird? The pair walked over to the guests of honor and offered their congratulations.

"My...*our* present to you." Carissa pulled out a small box. Cameron shifted his eyes between Carissa and the present. It may have been small, but Carissa knew it would be well received.

Hela undid the ribbon excitedly and tore at the paper. "Aww!" she squealed. "You remembered!"

Cam slanted forward to get a better view. Hela scooped the contents out of the box. It was a set of rings, fused together in an infinity loop. Hela explained the sentiment to Fen and, by proxy, to Cam.

"I made rings for all of my friends when I was a young girl."

Carissa smiled. "Young girl" for Hela meant a hundred years old.

"It was just a hobby for fun, but Carissa nearly refused to take it, saying it was too nice a ring. In the human world, a ring that nice was usually saved for a wedding band. So, I gave her two and said that this was my very early wedding present to her. She replied I was more likely to get married first, and she couldn't afford to give me as nice a wedding present. She was my tutor for human languages and spells."

This earned a chuckle from Carissa. Hela referred to any use of technology in the human world as "spells."

Hela continued, "And I taught her a thing or two about fae magic. So, I said to her, then make it my wedding present to use your fae magic and create an unbreakable bond to represent my union and our unbreakable friendship."

This merited a smile from Fen and an odd look from Cam. She realized what he must have been thinking.

"Oh, the engraving is from Cam," she lied. Hela pointed to the names inscribed on the ring and showed them to Fenigar. Cam's look changed, but not to one she expected. She still couldn't decipher him.

The night carried on nicely. Carissa's parents arrived, and they exchanged pleasantries with Cam. Jack and Maren seemed to fit in well enough. They talked with the other guests, Carissa more than Cam, and parted a while as each grew interested in this or that conversation. About an hour into celebrations, they came back together.

"Look who I found," Cam said. Jane stood beside him in a complementary azure gown, long earrings, and a necklace with a beautiful pendant that showcased a tree branching out in the center. It looked familiar, but Carissa couldn't place it.

"Hello," Jane said meekly.

"Hi, it's good to see you out here," Carissa said.

"My father kind of insisted I attend. He pushed for the mayor to be invited, too." Carissa followed Jane's eyes to the table where Mayor Belkin stood near the refreshments, laughing with the hosts of the party. They looked less interested than the mayor was in the conversation. It was interesting to note the Everly's influence spread not only through Moss Hill, but to the Vale Woods as well. Was it their association with the Morrigan that gave them such weight in the fae community?

"But your parents didn't come?" Cari looked around. She wasn't sure what Jane's father looked like, though she'd probably seen his picture in the newspaper. There was no sign of her mother.

"No, they had to leave tonight for a…meeting."

"I hope everything's all right." She recalled Cam's information about the company failing.

"Yes," Jane was a little too quick to say. "Just business matters." She wasn't very convincing.

"Well, I'm glad he convinced you to come. You look wonderful," Cam complimented a now blushing Jane.

Carissa smiled. Cam was a bit over the top, but Jane needed to lift her spirits after all. They chatted a while. Carissa didn't realize how much she had let her guard down until she felt a pair of eyes watching them. She looked around, trying to find the cause of her unease. The source of it was unexpected. There was Varick, dressed in his guard uniform. She glanced at her watch. Not time yet.

Then, she saw that he, too, had a refreshment in his hand. Likely the elderberry juice instead of the wine if he was on duty. She expected the sidhe might be on guard but hadn't thought to see them at the party itself. If he was trying to blend in to watch her, he wasn't doing a good job of it. When he finally caught her eyes, he looked away. Was it her imagination, or did embarrassment tinge his face in the slightest shade of red? If she wasn't imagining it, he had been looking at Jane.

Carissa smiled again and rejoined Cam and Jane's conversation. Tonight was full of all kinds of revelations. Before the meal, Fenigar stood and clinked a glass with a spoon to gather all of the guests' attention. He spoke with no cue cards in his hands. It still seemed odd to Carissa. She had always known him to be shy, but now he was smiling broadly, standing tall, and speaking in front of a crowd without fear.

"I must admit I was hesitant to give a speech tonight," Fen said. "It's a human tradition, after all, and I am not human. Nor is my exquisite Hela. Yet, are we not, all of us residents of this magical countryside, bursting to speak when our hearts have so much to say? Emotion speaks words that cannot be translated to any known language, and somehow, miraculously, we find a way to understand one another. Is that not a miracle? I love Hela. This is not difficult for anyone to understand. Any who see her, all who know her, love her dearly. There is no wonder in this. Yet, she loves me in return. That's a miracle. And I'm grateful this miracle came true.

"I didn't know how to express my gratitude before, now I can see that there are no words and never will be. So, Hela, my darling, to show my love for you, my heart has painted with my hands the way I see you with my eyes."

Fenigar unveiled the easel. Gasps could be heard, and breathless smiles seen around the table as the cloth floated down.

Hela's was the loudest reply. "Oh, Fenigar, it's beautiful!" She kissed him and wrapped her arms around him as the table erupted into cheers and clapping.

Carissa couldn't take her eyes away from the painting. It really was beautiful. The skin was touched with some metallic property that glowed under the moonlight. The eyes were shining. The hair blazed like fire flaming down her shoulders. Even Hela herself, as attractive as she was, wasn't as vibrant nor full of life as her likeness was in the painting.

"I didn't know Fenigar could paint that well," Cari's mother whispered. Dorian shrugged.

"Neither did I," her father replied. Neither did Carissa. She was happy to see Fenigar and Hela so elated, though, and enjoyed the evening's festivities.

"This is just the beginning." Fenigar took Hela's hands in his own. "The home I craft for us will be without compare in any realm on this earth."

The crowd cheered at this. Congratulations were sent in the direction of the happy couple from all throughout the table. The atmosphere livened quickly with smiles and singing and dancing. As the hours drew on, Carissa looked with dismay at her watch. It was nearing time. The Sidhe Council wouldn't wait.

"Are you ready?" she asked her father.

"Let's be off."

"Not just yet." She led her father and Cameron to where Varick was standing. The sidhe raised himself to his full height, looking down upon them.

"You need not plead your case to me. The elders will decide your fate," he said.

"We're not here to plead. We're here to present evidence." Carissa stepped aside for Cameron to move forward. He strode confidently rather than showing any hesitation. Maybe he was making up for his previous display of erratic behavior. She also thought about Alden's warning. Cam might not know exactly what he was in for here.

Cari expected she would have to argue with Varick, but he merely eyed Cam warily and heard her out. At the end of it, he seemed to take forever making up his mind. Then, miraculously, he agreed to inspect a human for signs of fae magic.

"We don't have time to await the results," Father said. "We should go."

Carissa looked over the crowd of friends, each merrily enjoying the party. Tension clutched her sides and snaked its way around her heart. Yes, she was ready to protect them all.

Chapter 16

The Sidhe Elders

The Sidhe Council, also known as the Council of Elders, was solemn and serious by nature. Of all the fae, the sidhe claimed the oldest heritage and adhered to the strictest rules. For this reason, Carissa's father had instructed her from a young age exactly how to speak, how to stand, when to bow, and all the myriad of formalities she should know when dealing with this esteemed type of fae. Dorian reminded his daughter of everything he'd taught her while they walked to the council, which exacerbated the anxiety she was already feeling.

"Dad, please. I'll be fine." Carissa twisted her necklace between her fingers, betraying her emotion.

They came to the largest building in all of Mount Vale. It was a twisted form of tangled wood in the midst green grass and moss. It was also the tallest redwood tree in the forest. For any who had never seen a redwood in person, the sheer volume of the tree would be difficult to believe. In the human world, it was an impressive wonder of nature. In the Otherworld, the sturdy redwood structure rose like a monolith that still appeared as a tree, but with carvings and windows that proved it to be it otherwise. What would have been branches in the human realm were, in fact, gardens and meeting places for the sidhe. At the base of what might be the massive trunk, the doors loomed over Cari and her father. As if detecting their presence, they opened slowly, almost to another world all by itself.

"Wait!" a voice called from behind.

Carissa and her father turned to see Cameron running down the lane. Out of breath, he struggled to speak.

"What happened?" Carissa asked. She and her father waited to hear the results of Varick's examination.

Cam shook his head. "All he did was a spell and told me I could leave. He didn't say a word otherwise."

"No," Cari's father said, "I don't imagine he would divulge anything except directly to the sidhe elders."

"He's still back in the garden," Cameron said. "I don't know if he'll make it in time."

Carissa and her father exchanged a glance. If Dorian were thinking the same thing as his daughter, he'd be worrying about whether or not to trust Varick with Cari's fate on the line.

Finally, Cari said, "You'd better get back to Hela's party. Maren and John may want to get back to Moss Hill soon."

"I asked Jane to take them home so I could come with you."

"That's very sweet," Carissa said, "but you're worrying for nothing. I've talked to sidhe before, I know what I'm doing."

"Cari, I don't trust these sidhe. I should go with you."

"No humans," Father warned. There was no arguing with that.

"I'll be right here if you need me," Cameron said, waiting outside the doors. She thanked him with a smile, and she and her father entered the hall.

Inside, the hall spiraled, the center was a swirling staircase, and there were exits on various levels leading to different areas, perhaps the roots and branches of this dwelling.

Her father stopped her as the doors were closing behind them. "You've never talked to the elder council before. If you think it's hard to talk to a sidhe, it'll be that much harder to be in a room with the oldest of them. Be on your guard."

Carissa gulped and took a deep breath. She had to be ready for this. There was no choice. For herself and for Moss Hill, she kept onward.

They walked up the stairs for what felt like an hour, but in reality, it couldn't have been more than a quarter that. Time felt still here, far more than the slow feel to time passage that Carissa always felt in the Otherworld. When they reached the top, they were in the open air again, and they could see leaves all around them in bright green, like flakes of emeralds dancing in the wind. Had they shrunk? She felt no larger than a bird up here.

The floor itself was an amphitheater. The council sat in a large circle around Cari and her father. Carissa felt as if she were on trial. She turned around, greeting every councilor with her eyes and adding a curtsey at the end. Her father bowed his head to each. Each nodded theirs in return. It felt a little ridiculous, though she knew better than to ever ridicule a sidhe tradition. When the gesture ended, she looked directly ahead at the eldest. By rules of the council, Cari's eyes were not permitted to stray anywhere else.

"You are called here, Carissa Shae, to answer for the crime of murder. What do you speak on this?"

Her elf ears reddened and her mouth went dry. She swallowed, trying to calm herself enough for when she'd have to speak in her defense. She hadn't expected to walk straight into a trial. Wasn't this supposed to be more like a hearing? To show shock would provoke the elders and worsen her chances of a favorable ruling, so she kept her expression in check. Her father was silent, as was expected of him regarding sidhe propriety. Now was the time to show him that she was capable of defending herself.

"Esteemed elders, I come openly and free of guilt. My hands are clean of this crime. I trust your wisdom as my judges." She held her hands upward toward the sky and extended them, to show that she had nothing to hide per fae tradition.

"The death cannot go unpunished." This was an elder behind her, one of the younger ones of the council to have such a seat.

"It will not go unpunished," said the elder directly to the left of the leader.

"Further knowledge is required," the eldest said. "If you have it, speak it now."

Knowledge was the cornerstone of sidhe respect. They held knowledge as precious, but only certain kinds of it. There were many types of information they saw as useless, some they turned their noses at, and some they rejected altogether. While it could have been bravado to act this way, Carissa always wondered if this was because they had knowledge of another kind which took precedence over all else. In this case, the information they sought was of the perpetrator of Miss Morgan's death. Fortunately, this was news that she had.

"With faith in the wisdom of the elders, I offer knowledge freely and with sincerity. An ancient evil has come to the human world, and perhaps even to the crossing of Mount Vale."

"We know of this," the same elder who had spoken first said.

"One of your kind has reported it," another chimed.

An elder with silver hair and a young-looking face added, "The ankou was seen among the fae this very day."

"You must speak on this, Dorian," the eldest said. All eyes turned to him.

Why were they asking her father? Carissa realized almost as soon as she wondered. Someone must have seen Alden near her father's house. Why, oh, why did someone have to see him there?!

Her father replied to their question: "Wise ones, you are correct in this as all things. The ankou is a friend to all of us, though he takes our souls, he wishes no harm. This is not a nasty ankou. He is the soul of a human, descendent of a

Gwragedd Annwn. He is a friend to my daughter and came in the protection of a sprite."

The very first elder, who seemed to want to give Carissa a hard time, said indignantly, "You invited the ankou to come into our lands?"

This was taking a wrong turn fast. Carissa had to get it back on track, which was nearly impossible to do without showing the slightest hint of emotion. She swallowed her fear, but she couldn't speak until the eldest gave her permission.

He did so with a loud, bouldering voice. "Speak!"

"Honorable sidhe, without the ankou, I couldn't have gathered all of the knowledge, which I bring gladfully to you." This appeared to intrigue the elders. Some leaned forward, some straightened, some perked their ears. Carissa continued, "The ankou has seen shadows looming from the being which has come to threaten us."

"The threat is not the ankou?" the elder behind her said.

"Who is this being of which you speak?" the elder to her right asked.

"You will answer," the eldest commanded.

"Most wise, it is the Leanansidhe."

The sidhe didn't gasp. They never did anything so emotive as that. But they were silent and motionless. Their eyes were locked on her. They may not have been breathing for the lack of noise around them. Even the rustling tree leaves seemed to have ceased all movement.

Since none of them had talked, Carissa continued. "She has come on the pretense of being a human named Estella, but as she is not a shapeshifter by nature, she couldn't alter her face and feared recognition." Carissa paused. Since conjecture wasn't allowed in the courts of the sidhe, she couldn't say that she "believed" or she "thought," instead she said, "She did kill Miss Morgan for the reason of fear. She was afraid of being recognized, and there was only one in Moss Hill who knew for certain what she looked like." Carissa explained the true nature of Miss Morgan but was cut off.

"We know of the Morrigan." The elder to the left waved a hand as if it were nothing.

"But the Leanansidhe is not powerful enough to vanquish the Morrigan. This knowledge does not satisfy," the elder behind her said. What was his problem? Did he personally have something against Carissa or was he just a naysayer in general?

"The Leanansidhe has only two powers," another elder said. This one was in Carissa's visual field. He had a young face despite his silvery hair, and when he spoke, the voice was young, but the tone of it was like one who'd seen many ages. "She can bring to the surface any desires of the heart for being greater than one is, and she can realize that desire by giving the ability for the victim to achieve their dream."

Carissa knew all this. The sidhe should all have known it, too. It seemed like a meaningless recap until the elder continued, "She feeds from the heart's desire and kills when the blood of it is drained. Her method is not poison, and a wasted heart to her would be a loss in vain. Without these hearts for sustenance, she cannot live."

"The elder generously shares his knowledge with you. Does this change the outcome of your accusation? Tell us," the eldest said.

"Knowledgeable council, it does not. It remains true that the Leanansidhe is here. Her shadows trail even up to Mount Vale itself."

"The threat must be eliminated!" one of the elder's voices boomed.

"The knowledge must be verified," the eldest said. "We hear your knowledge, now we must see your proof."

They didn't trust her. From what her father said of the Sidhe Council, they only required proof if they didn't believe the speaker. Of course, they had accused her of murder, so it shouldn't have come as much of a shock that they would doubt her words. If Miss Morgan had been alive, they probably would have taken her word for it. Estella was this vampiric fae they described. It was so clear to Carissa that that was why Estella had killed her. Why couldn't they see that?

"Great sidhe, there is a human—"

The eldest interrupted. "We will not hear a human. Present the next piece of evidence." She knew it. Where was Varick? She didn't like the guard, but she hadn't expected him to just not show up. She breathed in and began again, this time offering the only other bit of proof she had.

"Superiors, the sprite, Chaos, has knowledge of the fae and can verify Estella is indeed the Leanansidhe. She and the ankou can show to you the shadows left in Estella's wake." Carissa saw her father turn his head sideways, and although he kept to custom and didn't break his gaze from the eldest, in her periphery, she could almost see the frown on his face.

"No ankou is permitted in this council! He is not welcome here!" the sidhe to the left of the eldest spewed. The others agreed with their body language, whether it was their heads bobbing, their scowls disapproving of Carissa, or their arms folding at their chests. Carissa felt her face growing hot and her palms began to sweat. She had crossed a line she hadn't realized was there. They had something against the ankou. Why? It was up to the eldest now to decide whether anything Carissa said would be accepted by the council.

He lifted his head and eyed her as if she were a curious subject. The minute he spent deciding felt like an eternity to her. His deliberation ended, finally, as he leaned forward and faced her father directly.

"One who befriends an ankou is not unheard of in history. Describe to us such persons as the stories convey. Be brief," the sidhe said.

Her father stiffened. "My superior, they are brave."

The sidhe leaned back. "Brave. Perhaps so. Then bravery must be met with bravery. Summon Varick to me."

A sidhe guard near the door of the chamber left. It was mere seconds before Varick entered the hall, and another absurd ten minutes before the ritual greeting ended and the eldest made his request.

144

"Varick of Vale, this half-fae has suggested the presence of an unseelie in our borders. What knowledge do you have of this?"

From one sidhe to another, the customary titles of respect were not necessary. Varick simply bowed his head and raised his eyes again before speaking.

"We have found unseelie magic on a person. Though it is not confirmed which fae it could be."

"She is the Leanansidhe, or so we are told," the elder said. He looked thoughtful, eyeing all three subjects before him. At long last, he gave Varick an order—"You are to go with Carissa Shae on the morrow and confirm this by day's end. Be warned that this one has befriended the ankou. He is seelie by her word, and she claims he can be trusted. Take caution, this knowledge is unverified. Verify it is the Leanansidhe. Bring her to us or bring us new wisdom on this matter. The discussion is over."

The three of them bowed. With the ritual over, Cari's new trial began.

Varick walked in front of them and Carissa had to hurry to catch up.

"Thank you," Carissa was able to say once she was one step away from him. Varick whipped around so suddenly she had to stop in her tracks.

"All I have done is find dark magic on the human. There is no evidence to say who put it there."

"You can't think that I—"

"I think nothing but what the evidence tells me. I do not know your guilt or innocence regarding Miss Morgan's death," Varick said. "But I do believe you are wrongly causing panic among the fae, and I intend to prove it."

Varick increased his pace, leaving Carissa to lag with her father. Cameron was waiting outside for them when the doors opened. Several sidhe watched him from above. Sitting on a root outside the redwood for so long would arouse suspicion all on its own, but Cam was also holding his phone up in the air, slowly moving it back and forth. Carissa realized he was just looking for a signal, but the sidhe wouldn't know that.

Cari walked up behind him and cleared her throat. He turned, startled. Then Cameron stood and put the phone in his pocket. "How'd it go?" he asked.

"Well," Father said.

"Not great," Carissa said at almost the exact same time. "I have twenty-four hours to prove my innocence while working with a sidhe guard." She looked ahead and gave a nod in Varick's direction. He was already at least thirty paces ahead of them, going somewhere she didn't know.

"Working with the sidhe, even in such a short time, may prove more productive than you think. The sidhe do not do any work halfway."

"Except Varick thinks I'm guilty."

"On the contrary, Varick believes you are innocent," her father said. This caused both Cari and Cam to look at him.

Carissa's mouth hung open in disbelieve.

"He so much as said I'm lying about Estella. You had to have heard him telling me that just now."

"That's my point. Varick may not believe your theory, but he's expressing his disagreement to you. If any sidhe believed a person was guilty, that sidhe wouldn't give the criminal the dignity of engaging in conversation with them. It would be disgraceful."

That was a different way of looking at it. By that reasoning, Varick had thought her innocent from the start. Yet the summons and the accusations really sent a mixed message. It only went to show that even among the fae, the sidhe mind was an enigma.

In front of them, Varick traveled farther and farther down the path. "Come!" he shouted. Cari looked at her father and Cameron and shrugged. At least he was on their side.

Chapter 17

Following Fae

"Show thee, ankou." Varick was hesitant to call on the ankou but agreed to the will of the council. He insisted that they do so in the center of Vale as a good starting point for their investigation. Carissa only had a pinch of the ingredients for the summoning spell with her, so she'd have none left if they needed to call on him again. At least, not until she had a chance to go back to the Seelie Tree. Cari's father had returned home to resume a search for information about the Leanansidhe from his records. The three of them remained out in the open, summoning a specter in the dead of night.

Carissa hadn't fully recovered from her fear of the elder council, and Varick standing over her shoulder glowering wasn't helping. Alden wasn't appearing and, given the sidhe's animosity toward even the mention of an ankou, she wondered if he was going to show himself now. Cam gave Cari an encouraging smile as they waited.

"He does not seem reliable. Does he always appear when you summon him?" Varick asked.

"Yes, always." Carissa gritted her teeth and stuck her tongue to the roof of her mouth to keep herself from being argumentative. She was in the mood to give him a piece of her mind. Her father had warned her against resisting the council's will before parting for the night. Varick didn't seem to need his sleep, and she was resentful already that he'd insisted on meeting Alden and Chaos right now instead of waiting until a more reasonable hour.

"Maybe you didn't use enough?" Cam's intention was plainly just to be helpful. Carissa knew that, but that didn't make her any less emotional.

"I used enough. I don't know why it's not working!" Cari snapped.

Cam didn't respond. Neither did Varick. In fact, they didn't move.

"Cam?" Carissa waved a hand in front of his face. No response. That couldn't be a good sign. She looked around. Was Estella nearby, doing something to them?

A voice came from behind her, giving her a fright. "Why did you summon me in front of a sidhe guard?"

Carissa's first reflex was to step forward as if to run, which resulted in nearly tripping over a stone.

"Alden! You really need to learn how to make a less creepy entrance." She turned to see the elder Everly sibling with Chaos happily sitting on his shoulder. The sprite was face deep in a cherry, happily chomping away with sticky red juice all over her face.

"Why did you summon me?" Alden repeated.

"We need your he—wait, what did you do to them?" she asked. "Did you stop time somehow?" She examined their faces and walked around each one of them, shocked to see them this way. Even Chaos seemed to take an interest now. She dropped the cherry and flew circles around Cam and then Varick.

"I told you, I don't have any power over time. I can alter perception. You're perceiving each other at different rates."

"So, time?" She had to argue with someone. This seemed like fair game.

"It's like the veil between the human world and the Otherworld. I can shift you between this time stream and a faster one, but I'm not manipulating time itself."

"So then time is different—"

"Carissa, could you stop avoiding the question?"

She stopped examining the frozen pair and straightened her back. Alden was right. Time, relative or not, was quickly going to waste. "We need your help." She explained the incident with the Sidhe Council.

"You shouldn't have mentioned me to them," Alden said.

"Yeah, I kind of got that impression. But why?" Carissa was genuinely perplexed.

"The sidhe are, for all intents and purposes, immortal, so when a sidhe dies, the grief is for eternity. Humans accept their mortality—the sidhe don't. They fight it, and they'll fight me to keep away from it. They're the only ones who can avoid, banish, or destroy the ankou altogether."

Carissa's face fell. She didn't quite know how to respond to that. He didn't seem scared or angry, just gravely serious. He didn't agree to help, but he wasn't leaving, either. He stared at Varick as if deciding what to do. Carissa had to say something, but what would make Alden risk everything and agree to help them?

"It's a lot to ask, I know. For what it's worth, I'd do anything in my power to help keep you safe." She realized how corny that sounded. She wouldn't be reassured if she were him.

He examined her face. What was he looking to find? Faith in her? Trust? Chaos fluttered over to rest on his shoulder again, breaking his gaze. Whatever it was he wanted to know, he must have found it, because he gave his reply.

"All right, I'll do what I can." Time began again or their mutual perception of time—whatever Alden wanted to call it.

"Whoa." Cam brought a hand to his head.

Carissa touched Cam's shoulder, seeing if he was all right.

"Alden!" Cam smiled.

"What trickery is this?" Varick grabbed his sword from the scabbard at his waist.

"Hey, wait a minute," Cam argued.

"He's already wounded the sprite. Do you not see the blood?"

"No, no," Carissa said. "That's not blood. Come here." She gestured to Chaos as Cameron handed her a tissue from the counter. For her part, Chaos thought the whole event was hysterical and was deep into a laughing fit from her perch. Carissa grabbed her and wiped her face with the napkin. "See? Just cherry."

Varick scowled but sheathed his sword. He folded his arms, examining Alden. A moment later, the sidhe's hand hovered over his weapon, and he continued around the corner. Carissa's instincts spiked. She felt the elf magic radiating from her heart to her fingertips.

"So, you're the ankou?" he asked.

Alden's only response was to fix his eyes on Varick with stark intensity. Cameron wasn't one for uncomfortable silences. It came as no surprise to Carissa he would move around the corner and make introductions as if this were an ordinary meeting at a social gathering.

"This is Alden. We don't really call him 'the ankou.' He's more like an old friend." Something Cam said seemed to affect Varick. He moved his hand away from the sword and continued to stare at Alden.

"Everly." Carissa thought he whispered the surname under his breath. It was a matter of fact recognition. Carissa may have only heard it because she was closest in proximity to him. Varick walked up to Alden. He didn't draw his weapon this time, but Carissa felt the tension in every muscle. Varick put his arm out, a palm pointed straight open toward the ground.

"What's he doing?" Cameron stepped in sync with Carissa and whispered.

As if he'd heard, though Carissa doubted he actually had, he said, "Show us the shadows and lead us to the Leanansidhe." He looked at Cari. "If the fae is actually here."

Herbs and Homicide

Alden waved Cam and Carissa over to him. They placed their hands together, Alden's hovered over theirs. A mist encircled them. The surroundings changed. The blue paint of the shop began to fade, replaced by the earthy hues of the forest of Mount Vale.

The night was dark, except for the faint glow of the magic flowers touched by nature faeries. If not for their various colors strewn across the shutters, it would be too dark to see shadows.

Carissa had never wandered the fae village of Vale when all others were asleep. It was eerie now. The homes looked like trees and stones, so much so that any sight of a window or door felt like an illusion.

Alternating between areas of light and darkness, the translucency of Alden's skin played with Carissa's eyes. Alden, ankou, Alden—if she hadn't known the true case, she might dismiss it as exhaustion. Carissa shook off the tiredness and increased her pace to catch up with Alden.

"Where are you going? Where are the shadows leading?"

"I can't see her shadows now."

"Then where is she?"

Alden kept moving forward but glanced down at her from the corner of his eyes.

"I don't know. I'm following Chaos's advice right now."

"You can understand her?"

"Apparently." He chuckled. She had to smile at that—an ankou following the lead of a sprite. Priceless. Still, finally, she had found someone who understood the nature faerie.

"What's she saying?" Carissa said. This warranted a hands-on-hips reprimand from Chaos. "Well, I can't understand you. Sorry."

Alden kept that amused smile as he replied, "The shadows are watching us."

"Watching us?" Her hair stood on edge. "What do you mean?"

"She's hiding somewhere near. She'll stick with us, I just need to catch a glimpse of her or sense her."

"We are wasting time," Varick called from behind. "If you are misleading—"

The area went dark. Chaos clung to Alden's hood and pointed frantically.

Carissa froze. She found she had inadvertently gripped Alden's arm herself. Upon realizing it, she let go.

"Is it her?" Cam asked. Without warning, Varick bolted down the street.

"Wait!" Alden called.

Now all of them were running, traveling haphazardly down paths with protruding footfalls and inadequate light. Carissa stumbled. Alden helped her up. She felt Cam's hand to her right, offering support.

"I'm fine, where did Varick go?" Alden whisked forward up the trail. Chaos was saying something. Alden held her out in front of him. "What is it?"

"Wrong way. That's what she's saying. This is not where Estella is."

"Found him!" Cameron called. Carissa and Alden turned. There was Varick, at a crossroads scanning the forest trail in multiple directions. When they approached, he picked an object up off the ground and held it in his hands.

"Did you see her?" Cameron asked.

"You're wrong, ankou." He looked at Carissa. "And you for helping him."

"What do you mean?" Cam pressed.

"There's no Leanansidhe here," Varick said. Carissa tried to get a glimpse of the object in Varick's hand.

"How can you say that?" she snapped in defense. "We've barely begun a search, and you saw her shadow yourself." Cari could only catch a glint of gold.

"The shadow I saw wasn't a woman." Despite what he said, Carissa could see it was a woman's necklace in his hands. Why would he lie about what he'd seen?

"A man?" Carissa looked at the jewelry. Varick simply pocketed the object and ignored her stare.

"Probably a fae out late and off to mischief." He turned and started walking back toward the redwood of the sidhe hollow.

"You're giving up?" Carissa yelled.

"There is no trail. I won't waste any more of my time on this." Varick increased his pace. Carissa looked incredulously at Cam and then Alden. Neither of them, it seemed, was going to argue. But Carissa wouldn't let it rest. She couldn't. It was her fate on the line, and possibly theirs for helping her. She hurried to keep pace with him and kept down the path.

"You can't quit now. The council ordered you to investigate. You barely followed the trail, you haven't even spoken to Chaos yet—"

She stopped. A wailing sound carried into the night air. Someone nearby was in distress. It was full-on sobbing now. Varick perked his ears at the sound. Alden and Cam stopped. They must have heard it too. As if in unison, each one of them turned as they identified the source of the sound. It was coming from Hela's residence.

Chapter 18

Missing from Mount Vale

"He's gone," Hela sobbed. The party lights were still on in her garden, but most of the guests had returned home. Hela's parents and a few of her friends were all who remained, huddled around Hela who sat at the large, empty table with no Fen in sight. Where Jane's tears had been a flowing river, Hela's were a hurricane. Sal handed her cloth after cloth, all different hues and shimmering as they fell to the floor, covered in her tears. He bent to pick each one up while handing her the next. "I was saying goodnight to Jane, and Fen was just at the edge of the garden, but he wasn't there when I returned."

"This girl, your friend," Varick said, "was she alone?"

"She left with Marnie and…um, Jack, I think?" Hela said between sniffles.

"Maren and John?" Cari offered.

Hela twisted her brow in confusion. "They're not missing, Fen is." Her eyes pleaded with Carissa. "I checked everywhere. He's nowhere to be seen."

"If he didn't go home, maybe he just needed some air," Cam reasoned. The way everyone looked at him suggested they neither understood nor agreed with his perception. "I mean, he might've just gone for a walk. Thinking things through, you know? Marriage, it's a big step." The more he talked, the deeper the looks of annoyance became.

"You might want to stop talking now," Carissa warned under her breath.

Hela continued. "He was staying with us until the wedding. He's been working on a new home for us." She broke into tears again. "Something's wrong, I just know it."

"If it helps," Barnaby, whom Carissa hadn't even noticed was there, came directly up to the group. His best suit, a tailored burgundy, sparkled under the strung fae lights. "I did see someone, or a shadow at least, near Jane. I don't think she saw. Whatever it was disappeared down the street right away or I would've warned her."

Carissa and Cam exchanged a look. It was likely Alden, but he wasn't saying anything. Since neither Hela nor any of the guests had shown signs of startle or distress, Carissa assumed they couldn't see or hadn't noticed the ankou standing at the far back of the gathering. Alden had disappeared entirely at first, then shimmered into view. He was a silhouette now, but Cari wasn't sure who in the group could see him. Varick didn't seem to give any thought to the ankou.

"Was it a man or woman?" Varick interrogated Barnaby.

"I don't know." Barn shrugged. "Maybe a woman, I'm not sure." Cari looked at Varick, vindicated.

Varick ignored her. "Could you tell where this person went?"

"I think they headed toward Fairfield Castle."

The sidhe guard looked ahead of him to where Alden stood. The two shared oddly similar expressions of doubt.

"Come with me," he ordered Barnaby. The leprechaun looked at Carissa, his brows pulled together before turning back to the sidhe guard.

Cari moved to follow, but Varick held a hand up to stop her. "Your aid is no longer required."

"But—" Cari argued.

Hela's father only seconded Varick's opinion. No one dared to argue with Rolin. Since he was agreeing with Varick, the sidhe didn't disagree. The elf leader left alongside the guard, presumably discussing tactics. It would be no wonder if Varick refused even his help.

Carissa steamed after they left. Her mind was racing. Annoyed as she was, all the events of the last few days were finally coming together. Things that were not obvious to anyone else suddenly became clearer than ever.

"Think about it," she said to the remaining partygoers. "We were all impressed with Fenigar's skill with the painting. We admired the eloquence of his speech. None of us had any idea he had so much talent, why? Because he didn't have the skill before."

"Hey!" Hela's tone cried offense.

"Sorry." Carissa winced. "My point is, that's what the Leanansidhe does. She gives her victims the power to do the things they always desired but weren't capable of. Fen was shy and never painted so well. She gave him the talent and confidence to give the speech and paint a masterpiece."

"Whereas with me, she made me feel despair about my lack of talents." Cam's eyes were downcast.

Carissa gave a sympathetic glance his way.

"But what does the Leanansidhe do next? After she gives them that talent?" Hela asked.

No one spoke. Cam shifted on his feet and pulled at his necktie. The looks on all their faces must have said enough for Hela to understand.

"You mean, she—oh!" Hela wailed. Again, she sobbed, making her way through cloth after cloth as Sal scrambled behind her.

"There, there," the elfkin tried to reassure her. "I'm sure Fenigar is all right." He raised his eyes to Carissa, presumably expecting her to jump in.

"The Leanansidhe kidnaps her victims first." She didn't want to add any mention of the vampiric nature. Instead, all she said was, "We'll find him before anything happens to him."

She gave a half-hearted smile, trying to reassure Hela while also wondering how she would accomplish a promise like that.

She and Cam left the party to reconnect with Alden outside. The path was empty at first until they heard a faint whooshing sound behind them. They spun in unison toward the noise.

"Seriously," Cam said, "do you not make normal entrances anymore?"

"Alden, I didn't want to say it to Hela, but the Leanansidhe usually drains her victims, taking their magic or life energy. It's like sustenance to her."

With a realization dawning on his face, Cameron said, "She did that with me. I couldn't see her, but it's like I felt her pushing me toward what I wanted, but then the feeling was gone I felt so drained—not just of energy, but hope. Oh no!" He looked down and brought a hand to his face.

"What?"

"I might've stormed into the mayor's office and demanded a raise and a higher position. I also might've left with the words 'One day, I'll be the mayor of Moss Hill instead.'"

Cari put a hand on Cam's arm. "I'm sure it wasn't as bad as all that."

"It was worse. I think he might've fired me. Oh, this is not good. What was I thinking?"

"You were under a spell," Cari said. "I'm sure the mayor will understand." Even Chaos had flown down from Alden's shoulder to Cam's and patted his neck softly.

"I'm sorry, Cam," Alden said, "but we have to focus on Fenigar now."

"You're right. A job versus a life, I'm with you. So, what do we do?" Cam asked.

"Would Estella have taken Fenigar to Fairfield Castle?" Alden inquired. He didn't need to say what could happen if Varick took his guards to the wrong place. Chaos piped up. Carissa waited for Alden to translate.

"She's saying it would be a place where he could use his talents, so she could drain him as he uses them."

Cari added her bit of insight. "He paints and writes. Though, I suppose he could do that anywhere."

"Is the castle important to him?" Cam asked. "It would have to be someplace that's important to him, where he feels he's using his talent most. I mean, that's how it felt to me, like I was being drained most when I was in city hall and...."

"And?" Carissa asked.

"And around certain people." He seemed to search her face before breaking his gaze to look down the street.

Cari didn't know what to say or show to him. She kept silent, though there may have been a hint of a blush on her cheeks. She reminded herself they had a more pressing issue to deal with.

"What about sites that are important to both him and Hela?" Alden asked. "Is there a special place they share?"

It dawned on Cari that there was such a place for Fen, a perfect one for Estella's purpose. "Their new home," she said. "He's building a new home for himself and Hela. It'll take a lot of his fae magic and artistic skill to complete it. It's just a construction site. It's unoccupied, so she could be trapping him there."

"We should call Varick back," Cam said.

"No, it's too late for that. He could be halfway drained already. We've got to get to him ourselves."

"You won't be strong enough to fight her as you are now. You're exhausted," Alden said. "All of you go. You need sleep, I don't." He handed Chaos to Carissa.

"No way," Cam said. "We're not sending you to fight her alone."

Alden scoffed. "A Leanansidhe is nothing compared to an ankou. She wouldn't have any power against me."

Carissa cradled her neck and twisted her head, feeling restless but not tired. "I won't be able to sleep anyway. I'd rather stay and help. Besides, powerful or not, you're safer going with someone than alone."

"Trust me, it's far safer for you this way." Alden faded. His skin first became translucent, then the skeleton vanished in turn.

"Great, there's no following him when he does that," Cameron said. "Do we get Varick or try to follow Alden?"

"Both. We split up."

"Wait, wait, wait." Cam stepped in front of her. "Look, it's one in the morning. You're tired, I'm exhausted, and we," he pointed rapidly between them, "are not equipped to arrest Estella. I say we go together, and I think the best bet is to get Varick."

Cari wanted to argue. In fact, she stood there for at least a half minute, pondering how to counter Cameron's logic. The only argument was that Alden would be fighting Estella alone, but as long as he was right about being stronger, he should be all right.

"Fine," she relented. "We'll get Varick and then go with him to Fenigar's."

It turned out they didn't have to travel far, as Varick was rallying more guards from the sidhe community. He was reluctant to hear her news, and Barnaby insisted he "saw what he saw." Varick, uncharacteristic of a sidhe, struck a compromise.

"Hadir, Stotan, you're with me. All of you," he pointed to five of the guards, "follow him to the castle grounds." Cari looked at him gratefully. As usual, he seemed not to notice. He walked right past both of them and straight on toward the construction site. Cari and Cam turned to follow.

"Escort them to their homes," Varick called to the guards without so much as a glance in their direction.

"Hey!" Cam said. "We're helping you."

"You'll only be in the way." He still didn't turn around.

"Leave it, Cam. He's not changing his mind."

Cari clenched her jaw tightly. Varick's smugness bothered her as much as it did Cam, but he was right. Cam or Chaos might get hurt if they went along. She'd rather they were safe.

She didn't want to sleep through a crisis, but she had to admit that exhaustion was wearing her down. Besides, it was useless to struggle. There was no getting away from a sidhe guard, much less the two of them trailing behind Carissa and Cameron. They'd follow them all the way to Moss Hill if needed, but Alden had stranded them in Vale since the car was still at the Seelie Tree.

"We'll go to my parents'," Carissa suggested. Cam, not having anywhere else to go in the area, accepted the option.

The way was as dim as before. The gloomy pathway matched Carissa's mood. She was irritated with Alden, irate with Varick, and downright angry at the Sidhe Council. Cameron extended his elbow, which she accepted. Walking arm in arm, their steps synced up with one another's. Chaos slouched against Cameron's shoulder as if it were a bed. If it weren't for the imminent danger looming over their heads or the two guards following them, it might have just been a pleasant night stroll.

"Alden and Varick are doing everything they can. No use worrying about it more tonight," Cam spoke softly as they walked.

Chaos was sound asleep when they entered the house; she nearly fell off Cam's shoulder at the sudden frightful appearance of a certain banged up spectral form. Alden, incapable of bruising, but with hair wild and looking out of sorts, appeared in front of them holding an unconscious Fenigar.

"Take him," Alden said. He and Cameron laid Fen out on the couch. The elf appeared to be drained and weak. Cari fetched the paper from her purse with the list of ingredients Nan had written out for her.

"I don't think your nan's tea is going to cure this," Cam said.

"I have to get back." Alden started to fade.

"Wait!" Cari's exclamation came too late. "If we knew more about how he found him, it'd be easier to help him recover."

"Nothing else to do now except try," Cam said. He made his way to the door as Cari raided the kitchen cabinets for the necessary herbs.

"Where are you going?" Carissa asked.

"To tell Hela. She'll want to know, but also, I think the head of the elves might have some contacts who can help."

Cari hadn't thought of that. Cam's insights always seemed to add to her perspective. Cari saw a light flicker in her parents' room beside the kitchen.

"My father might know a cure as well, but go. Hela should know that we've found her fiancé."

Once Cam left, Chaos started with her hand gestures again. She made a circular motion with her arms. When Carissa didn't get that, she cupped her hands as if holding something.

"A bowl?" Carissa tried, but she was lost. "Of course, I'll crush the herbs. There're a mortar and a pestle in the kitchen."

Chaos stomped her feet and signaled no as loud and clear as a sprite could do.

"I don't have time, Chaos. I'm sorry." The one and only person who could understand her had just vanished. There was no way she knew what Chaos was saying, and Fen needed help now.

Her father came out of the room. Once she explained, he searched through the old book. If there was a better recipe for fighting the Leanansidhe's spell, he didn't find it. With the herbal mix, she was at least able to get Fen back to stable condition. Hela and her family arrived soon after.

"Oh, Fen, thank goodness! Carissa, how can I thank you?" Cari looked at Cam. Both knew but were unable to say who really deserved their thanks.

"I believe our gratitude would be best expressed by my testimony to the sidhe elders," Rolin said. "You have nothing left to fear. You'll be cleared of all charges by morning."

Carissa was grateful, but her worry wasn't for herself. She explained about Varick being at the construction site of Fen's new home. She might have explained about Alden, too, except that she felt she'd already made a mistake in telling the sidhe about him. Hela's father issued some elves to help Varick in the fight against the Leanansidhe.

Once Hela's family was gone, taking Fenigar with them, Cari was able to relax a little. She was still upset she hadn't been able to get Fen back to full health.

"You did what you could. And Rolin's sending help, so Alden should be fine," Cam reassured her.

Carissa nodded. She was too tired for words as her mother came into the room.

"Get some rest, everyone," Mother said. "No more worrying tonight. There's always plenty to fret about tomorrow."

Despite her mother's repeated requests to come to bed, to which he kept replying, "In a minute, dear," Cari's father stayed put. He sat in the plump armchair reading his old books in the sitting room when she kissed him on the top of the head and said goodnight.

Carissa took her old room, placing Chaos on a doily on her nightstand. Cameron slept in the guest bed, which was just a hammock under the canopies of two sturdy oak trees. Cari doubted she'd be able to sleep, but she was out as soon as she rested against the pillow. As still as she was, Carissa was running in her dreams, being chased by, of all people, John. Next, Cari was shouting at Jane, accusing her of poisoning Miss Morgan. The vision cut to the strange woman she'd seen at the church. The woman chanted a hex to immobilize her while Varick placed handcuffs in on Cari's wrists.

"Arrest her," Dream John said. "She's been falsely accusing my friend of murder. Guilty? Yes, of course, she's guilty, but that's not the point!"

Carissa tried to shout but found the woman's spell too effective to fight off. The dream ended abruptly with the last vision being that of Estella hovering over her, knife in hand.

"Didn't think they'd really catch me, did you?" Dream Estella teased.

Herbs and Homicide

Carissa jolted up, inhaling sharply as if each breath was a stab. The room was empty, except for Chaos still sleeping by her side. Carissa's hands went to her chest, no wounds.

The only piercing object was the sun. Its rays cut through the curtains in wild strands of fiery light. Cari finally regained control of her breathing and shook off her fear. Her dream had villainized nearly everyone when there was only one killer to be confronted. If they hadn't already, then today was the day they would catch her.

Chapter 19

Chaos and Captives

Despite such little rest, Carissa was rejuvenated in the morning. She dressed in less formal attire than she'd had on last night and hung the dress carefully in the closet. Then, she went straight to the kitchen, looking for the necessary ingredients to summon Alden, but there was no mistletoe. She'd have to start carrying a pinch of the herbs with her in the future. As soon as she had the thought, she shook it off. Why would she think she'd need it in the future? Once they caught Estella, this would hopefully all be over.

She woke Cameron so they could get an early start to the day. They ate breakfast and studied more about the Leanansidhe from her father's collection of historical records. Her father filled her in on some of his reading from the night before.

"Why did the Leanansidhe leave Moss Hill?" she asked between bites of her toast and jam.

"According to legend, the Morrigan drove her away. She vowed to return upon the Morrigan's death," Father explained.

"Upon her death? So, she didn't threaten to kill her?" Cameron said between mouthfuls. "This is delicious, by the way, just the right raspberry to sugar ratio."

"What difference does it make?" Carissa asked.

"Too much sugar and it ruins the whole thing." Cam shrugged.

Carissa glared at him. "The threat, not the muffins." Cam smiled to show he was teasing, earning him a sour look. Carissa went on, "It doesn't matter if she outright threatened her, the point is that it's enough motive for her to want to kill the Morrigan."

"Still, the Sidhe Council is right to say Estella didn't have the power to vanquish her," Father said.

"Two hundred years ago!" Carissa argued. "She could have grown in skill or discovered some secret weakness. We don't know until we catch her."

"They might've already done so."

"Then where's Alden?" Carissa said. "Wouldn't he have come here and told us he was all right or that she was caught?"

"It's early, he might have thought we were sleeping. I get that you're worried, Cari. But a whole squad of elves and sidhe went after her last night. I'm sure Alden's fine." Cam put a hand on hers. It did comfort her, but a moment later she pulled away.

"It is not Alden that troubles me," Father said. "Fen didn't improve with the herbs, nor with elf magic. According to my reading last night, the Leanansidhe may be using a chalice or bowl to contain the energy she acquires from her victims. The spell would need to be broken on the container itself before he could recover."

Chaos flew up from where she was sneaking pieces of Cam's food away from his plate. She dropped the crumble of jam-covered bread and rose to where she could get Cari's attention. She placed her hands on her hips and made the same gesture from last night.

"All right, OK, I understand now. The bowl, that's what you meant." Cari nodded.

The sprite triumphantly floated back down to the table. She held her head high. Then she sat, ever so eloquently, beside Cameron's plate and bit into the bread she'd discarded a moment ago.

"Do you think they'd have found the container?" Cam asked.

"I think we should go by the construction site," Cari suggested.

Carissa's mother could no longer stay silent. "You've done your part. You've informed the council, and whatever happened to Fen last night—I do hope he's all right—the sidhe will know it wasn't you. You don't need to keep investigating. Let Varick do his job and catch her himself."

Father gave Carissa that warning look not to argue with Mother. Instead, he suggested that they head to Hela's after breakfast and check in on Fen. If he weren't well, Father would tell Rolin what he'd discovered, and the elves and sidhe would conduct a search without them.

Mother seemed to have no qualms with this reasoning. Carissa knew well enough that when her mother spoke her piece on a topic, she considered it closed. It was best to leave well alone from that point on.

The minute breakfast was over, they walked up the path to Hela's. Chaos seemed to pick Cari's father as her favorite companion today, as she perched herself onto his shoulder. She crossed her arms and looked away when Dorian passed by Carissa. Carissa chuckled under her breath. That sprite was spirited, that was for sure.

At Hela's, Carissa couldn't hold onto her smile any longer. The gate, which normally was strewn with vibrant vines, held leaves that were duller than Cari had seen before.

Sal opened the door as if it was far more cumbersome a task than usual. "He's not waking. We've tried all the magic we know."

Carissa reached for his arm and gave his hand a squeeze. "Don't worry, we know what to do. He'll be fine." She might have made that a promise, except that her father stopped her.

Elves were not inclined to make promises they weren't confident they could keep.

"I will speak with Rolin," Father said. "You go back to Moss Hill, and I'll send Chaos to you when we've made some progress."

The nature faerie stood tall and saluted as if she were happy to be taken seriously for such an important task.

Cari wanted to argue but really couldn't see what she could do that the elves couldn't do better. She and Cam had no choice but to make their way back to Moss Hill.

The conversation restarted as they walked to the car.

"So, I'm assuming you want to summon Alden as soon as possible?" Cam said.

"Soon as we get to the shop."

Cam took out his cell phone and waved it in the air again. He frowned. "There really is no reception out here."

"There isn't exactly a cell service that offers a good human to Otherworld calling plan," Cari joked. "Are you worried about missing a call?"

He slid the phone back in his pocket again and slowed his pace. "No."

"You're sulking," Cari pointed out. "What's wrong?"

"Nothing." He caught her eye and then sighed. "I had this feeling like I might've done something stupid yesterday. Then I remembered what I said to the mayor. I was just hoping…never mind."

"You're hoping he'll give you another chance. I'm telling you, you're worrying for nothing."

"Maybe. Maybe not. I guess it leaves me free to stick with you today. I mean, if you want me to."

"I don't know. I think the mayor will be missing his chauffeur."

Cam exhaled a short huff and looked away. Cari only caught a glimpse of his expression, but from what she could tell disbelief was written all over his face.

"I think you should talk to Belkin. Fae and human relations mean more to him than a little outburst. I'm sure he'd reconsider when he finds out you helped save Rolin's daughter's fiancé."

"True, though, technically Mayor Belkin did ask me to help you, so I would still be doing my job if I stuck with you."

A smile spread across Cari's face. "Come on, you're calling him as soon as we get to town and I'm not listening to any more excuses." She took Cam's arm and wrapped hers around it, and they picked up their pace. They were at the car in less than a minute. Cam's good-natured smile returned as they got in.

Once seated and driving, he caught Cari looking at him a little longer than she probably should have been. But her gaze wasn't for the reasons he might think. She didn't want to hurt Cam's feelings by pointing out she'd grasped his arm only to make their travel faster. It was imperceptible how Carissa used the elf-light to speed their journey through time. She should have explained she was using her elf magic. She didn't want to lead him on. A few days ago, she'd have thought nothing of it.

She almost wished Alden hadn't said anything to her about Cam's feelings. Their friendship was comfortable and pleasant as it was. Since Alden pointed out Cam's crush on her, she'd gone from not believing it to...to what?

Thinking of Alden made her worry even more. *Aren't ankous supposed to be immune to danger?* Apparently, even if he couldn't be killed, he could still be harmed. She realized her elf-light magic worked in a similar way in the sense that it didn't make her indestructible. She imagined that in the same way she could hurry their steps now, Alden changed the perception of movement through time.

The road was bumpy, causing the locket at her neck to jolt forward. She clasped it to keep it from hitting her. Doing so made her recall the pendant Varick had retrieved off the ground. It was gold, an intricately carved tree.

"I've seen that before," Carissa whispered to herself, searching her memory.

"Seen what?" Cameron asked.

She tried to place the necklace in her mind. It came to her then. It was the same one that Miss Morgan had tried to barter with the morning of her death. The sidhe would have confiscated it when they took Miss Morgan out of the shop. But she'd seen it somewhere else, too.

"Jane! It's Jane's. I saw her wearing it last night."

"What?"

"The pendant," she explained. "I think it was hers." She recalled Varick's expression when he'd held it in his hands. He'd asked Hela specifically about whether Jane had been alone. Why? "I think Varick knows it was hers."

"You think she's in trouble?"

"Or she's about to be. But, no, Varick thought it was a man he saw. He might just be concerned for Jane."

"Concerned for a human? That'd be new," Cameron said.

"Yeah." It really would be, but she didn't dismiss it out of hand. The sidhe may not have cared much for humans, but they did have an agreement to keep the peace between the fae and human worlds. She was sure Varick would honor that. Besides, since her father's insight into Varick's mind, she was beginning to think she knew less about the sidhe than there really was to know.

As they came closer to Moss Hill, Cam tried the Everlys on his cell. No one at the estate seemed to be picking up. They expected Fudge to answer, but no such luck.

Once on Gorse Street, they saw that the lights were off in Barnaby's shop, so there was no asking him about what happened on the search of Fairfield castle last night. Even Maren wasn't answering her cell phone, which was very unlike her. If Jane was in trouble, did that also mean Maren and John were as well?

"Who do we check on first?" Cam asked once they got into town. It was a good question. Her biggest concern was one she wanted to investigate on her own. Right now, that was Maren. Cari turned her locket to bring them out of the Otherworld.

"You make sure Jane is all right, I'll summon Alden and look for Maren and John. Call me when you find Jane." She and Cam parted ways at the Seelie Tree, where Cam's car was parked on the side of the street. Cam left with a final request for her to be careful, which she said right back to him, but deep down she felt that danger was coming her way soon, careful or not.

Chapter 20

Caught Unaware

The shop was quiet when Carissa entered. She went straight to the back counter to gather the herbs to summon Alden. Once she had the ingredients combined, she added the mistletoe and began the spell.

"Show thee—" The back door slammed.

"Windy out this morning," Maren called out from behind. Carissa quickly brushed everything off the counter to the shelves beneath. There was no reason to involve Maren—or start another argument with her about Estella. Carissa could hear her assistant shuffling about the back room and smiled. At least that answered her question about whether Maren was safe.

Maren appeared from around the hallway.

"Good morning," Cari said.

"Is it? I guess so," Maren said, seemingly dejected.

"What's wrong?" Cari asked, then it occurred to her that even though she was here, she might not be unharmed. Her thoughts went to finding Jane's pendant on the ground. "Did you get home all right after I left?"

"Yeah, fine." Maren slouched a little as she walked behind her to the tablet. She turned it on, just standing there waiting for the screen to come to life.

"Was Jane okay?" she asked. There was definitely something Maren wasn't saying.

"Hmm? Jane? She was upset, I think, with that sidhe—the good-looking one."

Cari assumed she meant Varick, though she would agree to disagree about his looks. Maren was on to the task of examining the order list on the tablet.

"Upset how?" Cari pushed.

"She tossed down that necklace. The one Varick gave her earlier that night."

He gave her the necklace? At first, that sounded strange, but then she realized, of course, he did. It was with Miss Morgan's possessions and probably belonged to the Everlys. But why would she discard it like that?

"Do you know why?" Cari asked.

"How would I know?" Maren huffed.

Cari blinked, shocked by her outburst. She'd never taken a tone like that with anyone before. As long as Carissa had known her, which was all her life, she'd never been a hot-tempered person. Carissa moved forward, reaching out.

"Maren? Is everything okay?"

Maren hung her head. She was showing signs similar to what Cameron had been like the day before. Had Estella gotten to her?

"Why am I only an assistant?"

Carissa's eyes grew wide at the question. That was Estella's magic speaking through her.

Maren didn't wait for an answer. "I've wanted to run my own shop for a while now, and I might not know as much as you, but I know enough to run my own apothecary shop." She straightened and faced Carissa. "I was talking to Jane at the party last night, and she said she'd invest in me."

Cari couldn't believe what she was hearing. If this were Maren speaking of her own volition, she'd hear her out with an open mind. It was almost too obvious she was under a spell. Perhaps it was Cari's previous experience with Cam, but she could almost hear a faint whispering, as if Estella's spell were guiding Maren's words. It even looked like someone was talking to her.

Cari said the chant that allowed her to see both worlds at once. There was no one there. She kept the vision active, though. She'd rather see danger coming than be caught unaware today.

"Oh, almost forgot, the best part is, Estella said you could move your apothecary shop to Mount Wale and exclusively treat fae customers. Estella's even willing to help you get started."

That confirmed it. This was the Leanansidhe at work. Fear faded completely from Carissa's mind.

"Stop it. Right now." She directed her anger and attention entirely toward Estella or whatever force was controlling her friend.

"Stop what? Cari, I thought you'd be happy for me, for both of us, really." Maren's perplexed expression grew as Carissa summoned the elf-light to her hands.

She ignored Maren's puzzlement. "Estella: Let. Her. Go." Carissa warned in slow, clear commands, though she wasn't sure whether Estella was listening.

"What do you mean?" Maren looked around. She turned her head from one side and then the other, scanning the shop. "Estella's not here."

Carissa recalled the tea Nan had made for Cameron. It hadn't been so effective with Fen, but then, it didn't seem like Estella had used the same spell on him. It was more like the magic being drained from the elf was being used on humans like Cam and Maren.

Cari had made extra herbal packets at her parents' house. She grabbed one from her purse and mixed it with water into a vial. She warmed it with her light magic and shook the liquid. Then, she sat a confused Maren down in the office room to drink the concoction. A few sips in, she grasped her forehead and began snapping out of it.

"How're you feeling?" Cari asked.

"Hmm?" Maren murmured. "This is really good." She took another sip.

If her reaction were going to be like Cam's, she'd be a little dazed for a while. The spell wouldn't wear off immediately, but at least it was starting to have some effect.

"Just stay here. I'll be right back." She went back to the front counter and finished the summoning spell for the ankou. She waited, but nothing happened.

Nothing, that is, until a commotion outside startled her. Cari expected to see Alden, but when she looked up, Varick, two sidhe guards, and Barnaby were standing in the street. She felt the immediate rush of relief. If Varick was all right, Alden probably was too. But before she could smile, she realized they weren't standing with Barnaby but looming over him. More accurately, Varick and the guards were arresting him.

"But, what have I done?" Barnaby asked loudly as Carissa rushed out.

"What's going on?" Cari asked. Varick ignored her. Carissa moved to stand by Barnaby's side. She insisted with more tenacity and stared right at the guards to show she wasn't going to back down. "Varick! The sidhe elders ordered us to help each other. Now, I'll ask again. Why are you arresting Barnaby?" Cari had no other argument to back her up and no power to stop them, but whatever was going on here had to be a mistake. She could feel her heart pumping fast and the elf-light tingling at her fingertips. Alden might be able to help her defend Barn. Why wasn't he appearing? Was Alden that afraid of the sidhe? Or, was he in trouble?

Varick sneered. "This hooligan lured my guards into a trap at Fairfield Castle. He deliberately took them to an area of the castle where he'd damaged the wall and caused it to collapse on them."

"I'm sure it was just an accident." Carissa was floored they would blame something like that on Barnaby.

"What wall? Fairfield Castle, what are you talking about?"

"Don't deny the allegations. One of my best saw you with his own eyes using magic on the wall."

"That's impossible!" Barnaby argued.

"Of course it's impossible," Cari said. "You can't really believe he would do something like that!"

"You mean to say my guard is a liar?" He said it calmly, but Cari knew all too well the pride of a sidhe. This would cross a line from which she would never recover. She might be banned from the Vale woods altogether if she didn't backtrack, and quickly.

"I'm only saying I'm sure there's an explanation. Maybe he saw it falling and was holding it up?" She looked at Barnaby, hoping he would corroborate her suggested explanation.

"Well, I'll call him a liar," Barn said. "I wasn't even in Fairfield Castle last night!" The indignation in his voice was met with equal incivility as they bound the handcuffs with magic. Cari couldn't have been more astounded by both his revelation and their deafness to it.

"How is that possible?" Cari asked.

"He's lying," Varick said.

"But what if he's not?" Cari asked. "What if Estella, I don't know, disguised herself with some kind of magic."

"The Leanansidhe is not a shapeshifter." Varick moved to mount his horse. Barnaby was placed on a horse with one of the other sidhe guards. "Besides, we caught her this morning. She will be sentenced by the end of the day.

"You caught Estella?" Carissa was relieved, but only a little. There was still the matter of why Alden wasn't appearing and the fact that Fen hadn't yet been cured. Varick turned his horse with a sharp tug on the reins. They rode with fury.

"Wait!" Cari called. "What about Alden?"

She was beyond frustrated. She knew based on what her father said that Varick even answering her meant he trusted her. He'd ignored Barnaby completely. She could understand his anger at the thought of his friends being injured, but if only he would stop and listen! If he'd listened last night, he wouldn't have sent the guards with Barnaby, or Barn's imposter, at all. If he'd heard them out right now, he would see the possibility of a shapeshifter meant…what? Did it mean Estella had acquired new a power—one that might help her escape? Did it mean there was more than one unseelie in Moss Hill?

Whatever it meant, Varick and his sidhe guards were too far gone down the pathway to call them back to reason. Cari bolted back to the shop and thrust open the door.

"Stubborn, annoying, egotistical," she muttered to herself.

A loud crash interrupted her tirade. The shelves to Carissa's left came crashing down. Alden knelt, clutching his chest. Cari slid forward to where he was on the floor.

"I'm okay," Alden said. He steadied himself against the nearest intact shelving. They both stood up.

"Let me help you." Cari moved to the counter, though she wasn't sure exactly what to get. As far as she knew, an ankou shouldn't be hurt like this at all.

"There's no time," Alden said. "You need to come with me." He grabbed hold of Carissa's wrist.

"Wait, what's—?" Carissa asked, but they disappeared, leaving the shop unattended. They weren't there to see the front door open and a confused-looking John Goodfellow walking in.

"Hello?" John called. "Carissa? Maren? I can't find Estella anywhere. Have either of you seen her?"

Chapter 21
Freedom and Foul

"Where are we?" Carissa asked.

"Fen's home, from the viewpoint of the human world." Alden let go of her hand and led the way. Carissa had never seen inside the town of Vale from the perspective of the human realm. Here, it looked like they were inside a hollow. There was nothing but tree bark and leaves around them. Looking more closely, she realized even in this world the vines and open spaces were unnaturally formed.

There might have been a kind of beauty to it, except it felt like a curtain was blocking the light all around. They walked through to a larger space. Faint light shone from every angle above and to the sides, but it was still dim. The place was eerie.

Then she realized why. The house was building itself. The vines were spreading around the ceiling and covering the walls.

Hesitantly, she walked deeper in. "The chalice," Cari whispered, looking into a large, crystalline, vase-looking object across the room.

"You know what it is?"

"She's draining him, near as I can tell, of magic or life energy. I'm not sure which." She looked up at the ceiling. It was still forming the outside of the home. "I think this is Fen's magic. He's still building with his mind."

"What happens when the house is complete?" Alden asked.

Cari answered with a look—one that said Fen would certainly be drained when the home was complete.

"Can you break it?" Alden asked.

"I'm not sure. Possibly. I'll have to get a few things from the shop." She moved closer and reached out to the chalice.

"Don't touch it," Alden warned. "There's some kind of spell on it. It started draining me. It took a while to break free."

How long is a while? Cari wondered.

"Cari?" She saw her father walking in alongside some elves. "Ah, the ankou. Now I see. So, you tracked the magic here too." He directed the elves around the chalice. Chaos hovered directly over Alden. He looked downward at the sprite, who was now hugging his neck. Lifting his eyes back to Carissa, he smiled. "Well, Cari, since you're here, how about giving us a hand?"

Alden shifted his gaze downward before putting his focus on the elves. Cari turned her attention to her father and asked, "Of course, what can I do?"

"Take out that device, what is it called?"

She smiled again. Fae didn't use technology. No matter how many times she told her father what it was or how fascinating he found it, he never remembered what it was called. "My phone?"

"Right, take it out, and write this down." He and the other elves examined the chalice, listing components of the spell and what they would need to break it. She wrote diligently. Chaos moved from one elf to another, peering over everyone's shoulders.

When the list was done, Alden transported her back to the Seelie Tree Apothecary. Chaos stayed back with Cari's father as the elves continued trying to slow the spell.

Inside, Carissa hurried straight to work. She put the phone down on the counter.

"Is that you, Carissa?" Maren came out of the back room, followed by John.

"What's going on?" John asked.

"You!" Maren exclaimed. "Cari, it's that guy I saw when Miss Morgan—"

"I don't have time to explain," Cari said.

"Is everything all right?" John asked.

"Fen's in trouble." Carissa bit her lip and stopped what she was doing. "John, I don't know how to tell you this, but, Estella—"

"I know." John looked down. He rubbed Maren's arms. "Maren told me. I could see she was under some kind of…wow, I can't believe I'm about to say this…she was under some kind of spell."

"Cari, I'm really sorry," Maren started.

"It's OK." Cari put up a hand. "But whatever spell she had on you, she's got a much stronger one on Fen."

Alden spoke. "We have to put together the herbs on her list for the counterspell."

"Can we help?" John asked.

Carissa didn't waste a second. "If you both want to help, go as quickly as you can." She ordered all three of them to collect ingredients from the store shelves, trying her best to create a spell to counteract Estella's magic. Not knowing how the spells worked, Carissa added a few extra ingredients on the side to improvise on the spot if needed.

She instructed them to gather the freshest herbs they could find, hoping the strength of the spell would be enough to release Fen. Once the ingredients were all collected, she began crushing them into a fine mix.

"Wait—this isn't nasturtium, this is poppy." Carissa pushed the red flower aside and gestured to Alden, who was standing near the baskets of herbs. "The orange one." It was hard enough doing the spell without inexperienced helpers.

"Sorry," John said, "I think that was me. I don't know these flowers so well."

"It's all right." Carissa tried to keep the edge out of her voice. Time was running out. She put the last of the crushed herbs into the mix. "I think we're done."

"That's it?" John asked. "Isn't something supposed to happen? Something magical, I mean?"

"Not here, but there will be. Ready?" Carissa asked Alden. He took her hand.

"Can we come?" John asked.

"It's too dangerous," Alden said.

"Sorry," Cari added before they disappeared.

Back in Fen's construction site, the elves had made some progress. They looked somewhat relieved. Cari handed them the bag of herbs. Her father took them and kept hold of her hand. "With me," he said.

He poured the herbs into the chalice and put both their hands atop the flame that the reaction of magic and herbs created. Carissa followed suit with her father and the other elves, allowing the elf-light to pass through her into the goblet. The flames intensified to a white light.

"Now watch," her father said. They all pulled their hands away.

"What are we waiting for?" Cari whispered.

"Macara is with Fen. She's breaking the binding on the other end of the spell."

"Macara?"

"Miss Morgan's sister," he replied.

The flames burned blue, shrunk, and then died completely.

A collective sigh of relief could be heard between all of them. It was over. Yet, when she looked at Alden, she recalled there was still someone very much in trouble at this moment.

Chapter 22
Mayoral Mayhem

Barnaby was still in the custody of the sidhe guard. Varick had retired for the morning, which Carissa understood after the perilous night without rest. As the head guard on this case, though, Varick had to be present for all visitations or pleas. This meant nothing could be done for Barnaby while he was off duty.

Carissa had wanted to see Miss Morgan's sister, but by the time she reached Hela's home, Macara had already left "to attend to other matters." Carissa brooded back in her own home while Alden left to find Macara. Since neither she nor Maren was up to working today, the Seelie Tree closed for the second time in two weeks.

Nan canceled her poetry club meeting, and the food that would have gone to her guests was devoured by Carissa, Cam, Maren, and John. Cam ate ravenously, Maren and John nibbled heartily, but Carissa's appetite was stifled. At her core, something still seemed wrong.

"Well, Cari, if you ever tell me about one of your gut feelings again, I'm following it. No questions asked," Maren said.

"Huh? Why would you say that?" Carissa was thinking of her own preoccupation with the feeling bubbling up in her stomach right now.

"I should've believed you. I don't know how you knew, but you knew she was off. That's a gift."

"I wish I'd known," John lamented, reaching an arm protectively over Maren. "Do you think she was pretending before, you know, at the college? Or do you think the real Estella is out there somewhere?"

"Either is possible," Carissa said.

"You should check." Maren moved a hand to squeeze John's arm. "It might help you, either way, just to know."

John smiled, tightening his grasp.

"Why didn't we think of that?" Turning to Carissa, Cam said, "If there's a real Estella, it would've been easy to check, and if the real one were still in the States, we would've known for sure that this one was an imposter."

"Live and learn, I guess," Maren said.

"At least we know what to do next time." Cam shrugged between bites.

"Do you think there will be a next time?" John asked.

"Let's hope not," Nan said, bringing the desserts over to the table. "What matters is you're all safe and sound, but I think I'll see about talking to the mayor and your parents. We might think about better security. Maybe the fae and human worlds could come together to create some kind of protection against the unseelie." Nan looked at Carissa and pursed her lips. "I'll talk to the mayor into fighting for Barnaby's release, too."

"The mayor?" Cari asked. "But Nan, Mount Vale isn't Belkin's jurisdiction. I don't think the fae will let him get involved."

"They will when it's a Moss Hill's citizen whose life is at stake."

"What do you mean?" Cari asked.

"Barnaby's a citizen of Moss Hill?" Maren put together what Nan was saying.

Nan smiled, sipping her tea.

"Since when?" Cari squinted her eyes at Nan's quirky expression.

"Since a certain prank got him kicked out of Vale. It was before you were born, and probably better left forgotten. As I recall, it was Miss Morgan who stood up for him and eventually persuaded the mayor of Moss Hill at the time to take him in— with the caveat that she would be watching him."

That explained Barnaby's complicated relationship with Miss Morgan. Gratitude and fear, it was an interesting mixture that brought amusement to Carissa's lips.

"That's great," Cam said. "I'll make sure Mayor Belkin knows about Barnaby's arrest."

Cari could finally take a bite of her Bundt cake and enjoy it, knowing that Barnaby had a chance.

"You've been rehired, I take it?" Cari asked.

Cam smiled. "I've been at work all morning."

"I thought you texted me that you were at Jane's?"

"We were."

"You and the mayor were at Jane Everly's? What for?" John asked.

Cam wiped his mouth. "Can't talk about it."

"Since when?" Cari nearly choked on her cake. Her mouth hung open at the thought of Cameron keeping a secret.

"Since he promoted me to Ambassador of Mount Vale."

Carissa laughed, earning herself a sideways glance from Cam. "Sorry, that's wonderful," she said. "Really, I mean it."

Even Maren added a "good for you, Cam."

"I hope Jane's all right," John said. They all looked at him. "I just mean, the last time the mayor visited you it wasn't for the best of circumstances."

"It's not her," Cam said. "It's something to do with her business, but that's all I can say."

The discussion dropped for a while, but Cari kept replaying events in her mind. She had the nagging feeling she'd missed something.

As soon as she was finished with dessert, Carissa wiped her mouth with a napkin and excused herself. She walked out to the garden, mindlessly wandering between the flowers and herbs. The nature faeries encircled her. Hiya and Cynth sat at the edge of a rhododendron bush with Chaos in front of them, moving her hands about, apparently telling them the story of what had happened today.

Carissa rested one arm against her diaphragm and put the other to her chin, walking in deep contemplation. She thought back to Sal's odd behavior on her first visit to Vale. Then, her mind went to Barnaby's statement that he hadn't been in Fairfield Castle last night. She knew both Barnaby and Sal too well to suspect that they were in any way involved in Estella's antics. Varick had been adamant that she wasn't a shapeshifter. If not, that could only mean that she hadn't come to Moss Hill alone.

Cari realized the only other fae who'd come to their unassuming countryside in the last few days was Miss Morgan's sister. She could be in Moss Hill right now, but where? She could only think of one place she might have to visit. Carissa stopped halfway through the gardenias, coming to a decision. It was time for her to meet this Macara.

"Hey." The back door slid open. Cam stepped through. "What are you doing out here alone?"

Carissa swirled around and hurried back to the patio and up the steps, past Cam into the house.

"Where are you going?"

"Out," she said. Then, seeing the four sets of eyes on her, she softened. "I just need a little air," she lied. What she really needed was answers.

Chapter 23

Meeting Macara

Cameron caught up with her outside. "Wait. I think I know where you're going." He pulled the keys out of his pocket. "I'll drive."

"Where is it you think I'm headed?" Cari asked as he opened her door. Walking around to the driver's side, Cam started the ignition.

"Jane Everly's, and for good reason."

"Why's that?"

"I didn't want to say this in front of the group. It would only upset your nan." If he thought Nan was easily upset about anything, he didn't know her well as he should. Carissa let that go, though. "That meeting away from home that her parents had to go to last night, it was to meet with the family of a traveler whose body they just found on the Everly Express."

"A body?"

Cam nodded. "They had to shut down the travel line, and the family is threatening to sue."

"That explains the woman," Cari said.

"Who?"

Carissa realized she hadn't told Cameron about the woman Maren suspected of being Miss Morgan's murderer. She explained how there was a woman with the Everlys, but it was likely she was just a lawyer, helping the family with their legal troubles.

"They're investigating who it is," Cam said, "but according to Jane, Miss Morgan's sister came here to investigate a shapeshifter, not the Leanansidhe."

"So, there is another unseelie in Moss Hill," Carissa reasoned. No wonder Cam hadn't seemed worried about the leprechaun. If the sidhe respected the Morrigan as she thought they did, all they needed to free Barnaby was to hear from Miss Morgan's sister that he was innocent. This made her feel better as they pulled around the Everly's driveway. Now she wondered why they were here, given that Macara might be in Mount Vale.

The butler, whose name Carissa recalled was something chocolate related but couldn't quite remember, answered the door to the Everly Estate. The wood creaked eerily in a tone Carissa hadn't noticed before. She followed the man down the hall, this time to the right. The hall opened into a large living room with a giant television, an ornate coffee table, and a plush, luxurious leather couch.

Seated there was Jane and, to Carissa's surprise, the woman from the church. If it was the lawyer, shouldn't she be with Jane's parents negotiating on their behalf? She and Jane both stood on, noticing the newcomer to the room.

"Miss Carissa Shae," the butler announced.

"Thank you, Fudge," Jane said in her kind, soft voice. Then she walked to Carissa to greet her. "Long time no see." She smiled at Cam. "Cari, I heard about what happened. Are you all right?"

"Are you?" Carissa said. She glanced between her friend and the woman. Jane tilted her head; her eyebrows came together. Then she looked at her other visitor, seeming to understand, at least in part.

"Oh," she said, "this is Macara." Carissa could hardly believe it. This was Miss Morgan's sister?

The woman took a step forward. "I've wanted to meet you." She extended a hand. Reluctantly, Carissa took it. Macara didn't let go. Instead, she clutched her hand between both of hers and leaned in. "You and I have much to discuss."

Carissa's eyes narrowed, trying to assess the woman's tone of voice and appearance. Up close, she had a presence about her that was definitely fae, but she looked and sounded nothing like Miss Morgan. She was gentle-natured and polite, tall and stunningly beautiful. Aside from the raven-black hair, there was no family resemblance. Vaguely, she recalled the Morrigan were shapeshifters too. It was an unsettling realization.

Macara also offered a hand to Cam, which he shook with a questioning look toward Carissa. He had no way of knowing Macara's real identity, and Cari couldn't exactly blurt it out. That would be rude. Rude was the last thing she wanted to be to someone like the Morrigan. The four of them sat, and Jane offered tea, which Carissa politely declined.

"I'm glad you're safe," Jane said, "and Maren and Fen, too." Macara had apparently told her what had happened at Fenigar's house.

"Speaking of Maren," Carissa asked the first question she'd come to inquire about, "I heard you had a deal with her to purchase the apothecary shop?"

"The apothecary shop?" Jane appeared genuinely shocked. "She asked for a loan. She said she'd been considering starting a business for a while now. I told her I'd hear her proposal and would be happy to invest, but I had no idea it was the Seelie Tree."

"It was, but it's a false alarm. She was under Estella's spell," Cari clarified.

"You may not want to dismiss Maren's request so easily. The Leanansidhe brings out ambitions already in a person's heart, however deeply buried. Though, she tends to use those ambitions for her own purposes."

"What purpose would she have for Maren to run an apothecary shop?" Cam asked.

"That's the question." Macara sipped her tea. She almost reminded Carissa of Nan.

At that moment, Cari noticed the broach on the table sitting between Macara and the young Miss Everly.

"So, Varick was able to return that to you?"

Jane's face paled as she looked at the broach. Macara spoke instead. "Jane, thank you for your hospitality."

"Thank you," Jane replied. "Oh, and you, Cam, for yours' and the mayor's help this morning."

Macara rose. "Will you walk with me a while, Carissa? I'd appreciate the company."

Cari hesitated. She was glad Cam was with her, but Macara turned down his company, asking again specifically for hers. She had no idea what Macara's intentions were or just how much power she had in her possession.

"I'll get the car," Cam said. "I'll meet you at the end of the driveway," he whispered, walking past her.

"You're all leaving so soon?" Jane asked. She tried to smile, but her eyes were glistening.

"They'll come another time again. This time, they came to see me, I think." Macara looked to Carissa for a sign she was correct.

Deciding her need for answers outweighed her fear of being alone with Macara, Cari stood too. She walked with Macara out the front door.

"Jane is not well lately," Macara said. "She has so many reasons for her sadness, but she's young, and with her whole life in front of her, she'll be more than fine. I daresay she may even one day be happy." Carissa could see her smiling. There was nothing about Macara to provoke suspicion, except Carissa suspected she was Macha but hadn't yet confirmed it.

The two women came upon a black dog directly in their path. Cari froze. She recognized the bulky animal as the same one who'd visited her home. She found she could hardly breathe, but Macara was unphased.

Instead, she bent forward and patted her own leg. The dog came to her. Carissa's eyes widened. She stared at the dog and its owner.

"The Black Dog of Death. It's yours?" Carissa asked. She'd never heard of a fae or human who could control this type of creature.

"The barguest," Macara corrected, "is no one's."

The dog, though monstrously large, seemed far less threatening in Macara's hands. Still, Carissa kept her distance. This was something from the realm of the ankou. Carissa wondered if even Alden could control it.

"It comes to you like a pet."

"It comes to me as a friend. It came to mourn my sister's death on the night of her passing."

"Miss Morgan was the Morrigan," Carissa felt odd saying it aloud. "As are you?" By fae standards, it might have been rude to say. She hoped Macara understood her curiosity.

Macara looked thoughtful, then smiled. "I think they referred to us as that the last time we were all three here. It was so long ago, I can hardly remember."

Carissa recalled the Moss Hill Fae Archives. It mentioned the Morrigan as a triple goddess. One of them alone, though strong, didn't constitute the entirety of their power. It was split between three sisters: Morrigan, Badh, and—

"Macha." Carissa identified the woman with her proper name.

A gust of wind passed through the air, tousling the woman's black hair. She placed a finger to her lips. "Some things are best left unspoken."

Carissa looked between the barguest and the priestess.

"Myth says the barguest comes when a person of great prominence passes. I know she was the protector of Moss Hill. We're without her now." Cari relaxed into the conversation. She'd never conversed this easily with Miss Morgan.

"Yet Moss Hill is not without a protector," Macara assured her.

"So, then you'll stay?" Carissa asked. She felt as if Moss Hill would be safer with Macara's presence.

"I may, for a while, but even without me, it seems there are those who will step into the role quite nicely."

"If you're talking about me...." Carissa shook her head, leaving the sentence there.

"From what I've seen of Moss Hill, it's not one person, but the strength of many that protect it. Still, you'll need help. The unseelie are drawn here now, though even I'm not sure why."

"The shapeshifter—is he still in Moss Hill?" This was the question Carissa had wanted to ask the most.

"I believe so. I've been tracking a hobgoblin for some time."

"A hobgoblin?" Cari shuddered. She vaguely remembered Estella referring to a hobgoblin the night she arrived in Moss Hill. Had they been working together?

"He's using some powerful magic," Macara said, "stolen magic, I should think, to conceal himself. But he's liable to be anyone anywhere."

"He needs to steal magic to conceal himself?"

"The Leanansidhe needs to drain a person to sustain her magic and loses it quickly. A hobgoblin can drain one person and live off it for months. But, because hobgoblins don't need the magic as much, they can be slower and more careful in planning their schemes. Even among the unseelie, he's not to be trusted. He'd steal the magic from any unseelie he works with as easily as if he were to steal from an unsuspecting human or fae."

Cari felt a chill run down her spine. "Do you have any idea who it is?"

"That's the tricky part. A hobgoblin can conceal its power. Hobgoblins essentially become the form they take, to all appearances. It would be difficult for me to recognize them, but if they recognize me, they would surely run. I was never one to hide among others the way my sister did. I'm not looking for the same type of awe and wonder I used to receive, but I would never bind my powers. It would only keep me from finding the unseelie."

"But wouldn't it be better for the unseelie to know you're here? It might keep them from staying in Moss Hill."

"It might, or it might cause them to target Moss Hill all the more. It's not unprecedented for them to go looking for a fight." Macara smiled. "Right now, I'm set to meet the Sidhe Council to pardon your friend, and I haven't the slightest doubt Moss Hill is safe in your hands."

"My hands? I don't think so."

"But I do, and not to lord my acquired years of wisdom over you, I think my years give me a bit of an advantage in my opinion."

"So, that's it? There's a hobgoblin in Moss Hill, and I have to figure it out myself?"

"You found out Estella fairly easily. I think you'll find out soon. You might even already know who it is," Macara said.

"How? Is this a test? Because I'd really prefer if you'd just tell me."

"I can't tell you what I don't know. I can only guess. Right now, I'm guessing with a little thought, you'll find you have gathered enough information to know who is. Just listen to what your inner voice is telling you." They came to the end of the drive, right up to the passenger seat of the car. Cameron looked a bit unsure what to do, especially when he spotted the black dog walking beside them. Maraca started to walk away.

"Wait," Carissa said.

Macara turned back. "Even I don't want to keep the Sidhe Council waiting, Cari. Surely you can appreciate that." She winked, then turned back toward the road and walked away.

Cari watched her disappear into the air. She opened the car door and slipped inside, feeling the weight of the Otherworld on her shoulders. There was a hobgoblin in Moss Hill? Compared to this, the Leanansidhe had been a walk in the park.

Chapter 24

Shifty Shapeshifters

Hobgoblin or no hobgoblin, if Cari wanted to continue to live a good life in Moss Hill, she had to run her business. Chaos insisted on going with her, which Carissa should have realized wasn't so she could be a helpful sprite. The nature faerie wanted a day of lounging in the chocolate cosmos plant on the back counter eating popsicles, and she made that known the minute they arrived at the apothecary and Carissa locked the door behind them.

"All right, here you go," Carissa said.

She grabbed the treat from the freezer by the door. Chaos snatched it eagerly, ripping into the packaging before Carissa had even opened it. The moment the wrapping was off and the orange popsicle lay across the soil of the plant, Carissa and Chaos both froze. There were voices coming from the shelves. The faerie and half-elf looked at each other. *Unlock the door and run or stay and investigate?* Chaos pointed onward. Against her better judgment, Carissa followed the order.

Her ears attuned to the voices.

"And we'll need more St. John's wort. Looks like three bottles are missing. Probably best to get a ten-pack on that, bulk is way cheaper."

That was strange talk for a robber. Besides, the voice was familiar. Carissa took quiet steps toward the back of the store.

It was Maren rattling on about the items on the shelves in the center of the store. Carissa placed the chocolate cosmos on the counter and meandered over to her assistant.

"What is going on?" she asked.

"Good morning." Maren was chipper. "Just wanted to help you restock, you know, as a thank you for saving my life and everything."

"We probably should've told her we were doing this," John stepped out from behind Maren, "so she could've slept in."

"You *didn't* need to do this." Carissa caught herself. She wasn't sure why her tone came out so tart, probably because they'd scared her half to death. She breathed out, reminding herself that it wasn't a hobgoblin who'd broken into the shop and that she should be relieved to see her friends helping out. "I have it handled, thanks."

The words still came out harshly. *Why?* A few seconds of thought was all it took for her to realize where her bitterness came from. Yesterday Maren had talked about taking over the Seelie Tree Apothecary, and today she was restocking the shelves without her best friend, a.k.a. *her boss?*

Carissa swallowed down her insecurity. Maren wasn't trying to push her out of the way, she was only trying to help. Carissa tried again. Third time was the charm.

"I mean, I appreciate that you're helping out, but I'm happy to do it. Honestly, it feels good getting back into work without…everything hanging over my head like it was the last few days."

"Well, in that case," Maren grabbed the pricing gun sitting on the mid-level shelf and handed it to Carissa, "you can label some of the items I took out of the storeroom." She smiled. "But we're not leaving. You never have to do anything alone. You can always count on me."

Carissa took the price maker. "That's why you're my star employee. Only, I think we should switch," she said.

"Oh, hang on a second," she said to John, recalling that he had been holding a notepad for inventory. "Let me get the tablet. I keep an inventory list on it."

"That's okay," she could hear John calling out. "I'm okay writing it out. I'm not great with technology."

She walked back to the counter and unhinged it from the console. Chaos was entertaining herself with a magazine that had been left on the counter. She hopped between the pictured pages and the popsicle, dripping juice as she went.

"That's Maren's," Carissa whispered. Chaos flew to the plant and turned her back while Carissa finished her lecture, "You clean that up and don't leave this counter until you do."

Walking back to the shelves, Carissa found John by the extracts and held the tablet between them, "You're doing double the work," Carissa said. "It'll be a lot faster with the program. Here, I'll show you."

She pressed the button, bringing the display to life. For a split second, his image on the black screen looked odd, causing Carissa to look up. She turned to him, but his face appeared the same as ever. It would take time for her nerves to calm back to normal after all that had happened. Macara's warning about a hobgoblin didn't help.

Thankfully, John seemed not to notice her stare. She instructed him on the basics and, though he was slow at first, he picked it up quickly enough to be a real help to her after the first few entries.

"So, have you seen or talked to Hela or Fenigar since yesterday morning?" Maren asked as they continued working.

"No, but I did see Barnaby on the way here. He says Fen is doing well, and the wedding plans are back on as scheduled. I wouldn't be surprised if we see Sal today even though we're closed. He'll have a lot to do considering he missed a whole day of preparation yesterday."

John had begun inventory on the other side of the shelf when Carissa noticed something off in the stock near where Maren stood.

Herbs and Homicide

"Oh, wait a minute, John. Did you add another order of datura extract?" Carissa asked before she picked one of the packages up and pondered aloud, "That's odd. I could've sworn I saw five of them." Around the same time, her phone chimed. She took it out, looking at the text.

Cameron Larke: *Found identity of a body on Everly Express: John Gosling.*

The phone chimed in her hands. The second text came through.

Cameron Larke: *Thirty-two years old, real estate investor.*

She stared at the screen in one hand, the datura extract in the other, thinking. There had been five only moments ago. Datura was used for divination or to enhance magical power. It was used sparingly, and mostly by fae customers. But, she realized, it could also be used for concealment. It would conceal a fae who didn't want to show their true nature—like a hobgoblin. She would have looked around, but fear paralyzed her and kept her eyes straight ahead on the label. She replayed in her mind everything she'd seen and heard in the last few days.

No one who'd visited the shop the day before Miss Morgan's death had proven to be guilty. Neither had Estella. Despite her being Leanansidhe, there was no evidence she had come to Moss Hill before yesterday. The day before Miss Morrigan's death, it wasn't just Barnaby, Jane, and Macara who had visited the Seelie Tree Apothecary in the afternoon.

There was only one other person besides her and Maren who would have had easy access to the ingredients behind the counter before Miss Morgan's death: John. Right now, a container of datura had gone missing practically right in front of her eyes. But there were only two other people in the store with her now: Maren and John. She knew Maren couldn't be involved in Miss Morgan's death, but had John been controlling her from the start? Carissa turned slowly and stared Maren in the eyes.

In a soft, halting voice, she asked, "Why didn't you want to work in the Otherworld the day Miss Morgan died?"

Maren looked a bit taken aback. Then, color flushed from her cheeks. "It's nothing, really." Carissa kept her gage. Maren's eyes darted about. Finally, she flicked them upward and said bluntly, "She told me to stop seeing John. She said he was trouble. I guess it upset me a little."

Carissa felt her own breathing stop. Slowly, she turned her gaze to the shelves. Could there really be a hobgoblin on the other side?

"Wait, why are you asking?" Maren glanced between Cari and where she was looking.

Carissa was keenly aware of John's footsteps coming around the corner, and her mind raced wildly, connecting everything. John came to see Maren almost every day at lunchtime. If not at lunch, he'd come in nearly every afternoon. Not only that, but he generally did come behind the counter to talk with Maren or even Carissa. Not once did either of them think it odd or stop him from doing so. John wasn't a customer or a stranger. He was…John. But, was he?

Carissa replayed events in her mind. Nan hadn't accused Maren but had pointed out that she was there all the time and had access to everything in the store. That would mean so did John. John was the one who knew Estella. John was the one who'd mistaken the poppies and nearly ruined the spell to free Fenigar from Estella's trap. John was the one who'd taken a vial of the datura just now.

"What was it you were looking for?" John said nonchalantly. He scrolled through the inventory list on the tablet, looking perfectly harmless. Carissa reached her hand out, beckoning for the device. He handed it to her. By all outward appearances, there was nothing to arouse suspicion.

Nonetheless, Carissa kept her eyes on the man in front of her. "John," she said, "where is the missing vial?"

John shrugged. "I don't know. I only see four, maybe you miscounted?"

"Or maybe," Carissa said, "you snuck it away from the others."

"Cari!" Maren came to her boyfriend's defense. "How can you say something like that to John?"

"Did you take the vial or not?" Carissa stared at John point blank.

Maren stepped between them. "Really, Carissa, what are you doing?"

"I asked you a question." She stood her ground, ignoring Maren and waiting on John's response.

"OK," Maren put her hands up. "The last few days have been stressful, you probably really did just miscount. Maybe you should go home and rest."

"I'm not going anywhere," Carissa snapped. Behind Maren, John's lips curled at a preternaturally slow pace.

Maren, unaware of his expression, kept speaking. "At least sit a while. Take a break. You might feel better after—"

"Maren," Carissa's tone cut through Maren's advice, "get away from him now."

"Why? Carissa, you know John." Maren's tone shook between defiance and fear.

"Just trust me." Carissa looked John right in the eyes. "He's not what he appears."

John smiled. Then he laughed, the scary, skin-raising, hair curling kind of laugh only an unseelie could produce. At last, he sighed, as if the humor were tiresome.

"Oh, Carissa, I didn't think you'd ever catch on."

Chapter 25

Unmasked Unseelie

"Wh-what?" Maren couldn't have looked more shaken. Carissa couldn't allow enough time for the surprise to turn to heartbreak as her friend realized the truth. She reached out and grabbed hold of Maren's wrist, pulling her behind herself. Maren, still in shock, moved with her guidance easily into place. The pricing gun dropped from her hands.

John made no move. He was more powerful than the Leanansidhe had been and there was no doubt he could combat any defense they threw at him.

"Stay back," Carissa warned.

"I don't understand," Maren muttered.

"Humans," John said, glancing over Carissa's shoulder. "They're always a bit behind, aren't they?"

Carissa put one arm behind her to touch Maren's arm. It was a gesture of sympathy, but there was more to it than support. Carissa's eyes flitted down to her side. If she could summon as much of her elf-light as possible to throw at him in one jolt, she and Maren might be able to run for the front door. But then Chaos would be left in the shop.

Herbs and Homicide

As if reading her mind, John taunted, "Tsk, tsk. I'm disappointed. I didn't think you were one to run from a fight."

He was baiting her to stay, but she wouldn't fall for it. She stepped back. Fighting a hobgoblin was never a good idea. She tried talking instead.

"You could have fought us earlier, but you didn't. Why?"

His lips twisted savagely. "I really didn't want to have to kill you. You know, your apothecary is the perfect means of infiltrating Moss Hill."

While he talked, Carissa handed the tablet to Maren behind her. If she could just be subtle enough to use it without John seeing, she could use it to send a message to Cam or the police or any one of the shop owners next door. She couldn't defeat John, but between him making his classic villain speech and her elf magic, she might be able to hold him off until help could arrive.

John went on, "You serve both fae and humans. They take what you give them without question. Even if you gave them, say, poison, like you did with Miss Morgan, you could charm them, enchant them, put them under any spell, and they'd still trust you! But you're more perceptive than a human. Maren, she'd be the better proxy. Far easier to manipulate. Oh, well." He sighed. "Now, I'll have to dispose of you both." He looked around. "It'll take longer, but I'm sure it wouldn't be long before the Seelie Tree falls into my hands."

He took a step forward. Carissa braced herself, putting her hands out in front of her. Waving her arms in circles in front of her, Carissa used her elf-light magic to create a makeshift shield. But John's magic wasn't like Estella's. It didn't come in blasts for her to deflect or energy that she could disperse. A green mist formed around her feet. She and Maren backed away, inching toward the front of the store.

John's devilish smile increased as the mist rose. It swirled around them, enveloping their feet, then their calves. It didn't matter where they moved. The fog moved with them.

"Do something!" Maren shouted. Carissa faced her palms downward. She tried to push the fog down. It succeeded in clearing a few centimeters of the hazy threat, but no more than that.

"I can't." Cari struggled against the darkening air. "He's too powerful." She tried again. For every inch of the cloud she was able to push down, it rose two inches more. She tried lashing out at John himself, but he deflected it with the palm of his hand.

"Ouch," he said, waving his palm back and forth. "That stung." Carissa tried again and again, but he deflected each time. The mist had risen chest-high at this point.

"I can't believe I'm going to die like this. You're the worst boyfriend ever!" Maren shouted, closing her eyes tightly. Carissa's hands were locked against the sides of her body.

She looked around frantically for anything that might help her defeat the hobgoblin, or at least delay him until the help Maren called for could arrive. Then she noticed Chaos in flight above John's head. She nodded, as subtley as she could. Chaos flew so fast Carissa couldn't track her. She didn't have to, though.

Boxes flew off the shelf and bottles shattered against the floor. It was a shallow thing to be angry about given the situation, but Carissa wished Chaos could find a way to fight John that didn't involve ruining more inventory. A bottle flew right into John's face and broke. It worked.

John's hold of them let up. Carissa quickly pulled a stunned Maren toward the door. The mist caught up with them in the entryway.

"Run!" Carissa said.

She tried pushing Maren out of the way, but the fog followed. The hobgoblin targeted the meek assistant. Carissa tried another shot. Chaos lunged at his head at the same time. Cleverly, the hobgoblin stepped back. A mid-air evasion caused Chaos to lose control of her flight. She went down.

"Cari," Maren's wavering voice grew shrill. She tip-toed one way, then another. Black mist circled her feet.

Rage swirled around Carissa's fingertips. Her elfish instincts took over.

"Aaargh!" Carissa's magically-charged hands thrust forward and she ran toward him.

The elf-light hit John first. Her hands met his hobgoblin power next. The force was uneven. He staggered. She fell.

John put a hand to his temple and shook his head. Maren took the opportunity not to leave, but to help Cari back up. She didn't make it. The black mist enveloped her again—much faster this time. Carissa hurried to her feet and found herself stuck in place.

She tried to leap, but it became a wild grasping for the shelves. When the room stopped spinning, the mist was up to Maren's neck. Chaos was nowhere in sight. There was no sign of anyone coming.

A half-whispered plea was all she could think to do, "Stop. Please, stop."

As if on command, John slowed until he was a still as stone, grinning deviously and holding an immobile arm out in front of him. The fog dissipated. Carissa found she could move again.

"How are you doing this?" Maren whispered.

Cari looked at her hands. "I'm not."

Maren was clutching the table wide-eyed, but unharmed. Cari reached out to her. She put a hand on her arm just to assure both of them that they were okay. Then she turned back to face their attacker.

John couldn't, and wouldn't, be doing this himself. The only person she knew who could make it seem like time had stopped was—"Alden!" she exclaimed, seeing the ankou shimmer into sight beside the hobgoblin.

"Cari, it's that woman!" Maren clutched her shoulder and huddled close to her. Carissa reached instinctively behind her to pull Maren away, thinking that somehow Estella had freed herself from sidhe custody. But, no, it was Macara. Not just Macara, but an entire band of sidhe, including one of the council elders himself lined the front of the shop.

The old sidhe walked to the hobgoblin and circled him, chanting something in a language Carissa couldn't understand. The other sidhe surrounded him, and Alden approached.

"Are you all right?" He reached a hand out toward her but seemed to think better of it.

"I am, thanks to all of you." She felt as if her heart must have frozen and had finally caught back up to speed. It thumped in her ears.

It didn't escape Macara's perception. At least she seemed to know exactly what to do to comfort Carissa. "Well done." Macara put a hand around either of Carissa's arms.

"But I didn't do anything, except almost die," Carissa argued.

Macara gave a gentle squeeze and then pulled away. "You survived a hobgoblin attack. That's more than anyone I've known who've had the misfortune to come across one. And you kept your friend alive." Macara nodded in Maren's direction.

Poor Maren. Attacked by a hobgoblin, saved by a Grim Reaper, and surrounded by sidhe guards, it was no wonder she was in shock.

"Maren," Carissa said, "this is Macara." She hesitated, how could she describe her? She smiled, settling on an adequate description, "She's a friend." A thought entered her mind as she said it. Maren couldn't have contacted Macara if she didn't even know who she was, and the sidhe didn't use human technology. Alden, well, he couldn't exactly carry a smartphone with him anymore. So, how did they know they were in trouble?

"A little sprite told me," Macara said. Chaos? How? There was a bit of gleam in Macara's eyes and a friendly smile on her lips as she said it. Chaos, who was celebratory-dancing on Alden's shoulder, seemed more mysterious than ever.

Macara turned and went to help the sidhe take in their next prisoner. Carissa watched her join the elder and returned the expression. A little mystery in Moss Hill wasn't always a bad thing, she supposed.

"Carissa!" Cam pushed on the front door but was locked out. Maren went to open it. "Is everything all right?" He was breathing deep and glancing between everyone.

"Yes." Cari laughed. "I guess Maren's message got to you a bit late. We're fine."

"What message?" Cam asked.

Maren shook her head. "I didn't send any message."

Cari's mouth hung open. "Maren! You had the tablet for *minutes* when he couldn't get a clear view of you! Why didn't you use it?"

"I did." Maren's tone was defensive. "I recorded everything he said." She beamed with pride.

"Recorded—what good would that have done us if we were dead!"

"At least we have proof of what he was planning!"

The two bickered.

"I'll take that." Alden held out his hand. Maren handed him the tablet, which he walked over to Macara, presumably so she could turn it over as evidence to the sidhe, though since it was a human device, Carissa doubted they would use it.

"Wait, if Maren didn't send you a message, how did you know we were in trouble?"

"I didn't, not until I got here."

"Then, and don't take this the wrong way, why did you come?"

"I was coming to tell you about another emergency."

Carissa's heart sank. "Oh no, is it Fen? Has Estella escaped?"

"No, no, nothing like that." He held up a long, rolled up piece of paper. Carissa took it from his hands and inspected it. It was a list of ingredients, mostly for recipes of classic fae celebratory cuisine. "Have time for a wedding emergency?" Cam asked.

Carissa laughed. "Absolutely."

Chapter 26
Weddings and Whimsy

Hela made a beautiful bride. In the backdrop of the setting sun, the faerie lights hovering above her, and the inner glow of her elf-light, she quite literally radiated happiness. Fen was the picture of contentment and Carissa was glad to see he had regained his full health in the two weeks after the whole dreadful ordeal with Estella. She was also delighted to see that Hela had invited a Moss Hill reverend to officiate the ceremony, which was far more like a human ceremony than Cari had expected.

"Did I do everything right?" Sal whispered as he took a seat beside Carissa on the bride's side of the family.

"Yes," she said. "To the last detail."

"Do you think Hela's human friends are comfortable?"

Carissa looked beside her to Cam, who smiled. "I think you did a brilliant job, Sal," Cam approved. Carissa and Cam kept their eyes on Hela as she walked down the aisle to the tune of elven flutes. An untraditional wedding song for either fae or humans, but a sweet choice for the occasion.

Carissa looked for Chaos, Hiya, and Cynth, who'd all been included among the nature faeries selected to hold the train of Hela's dress. Joy filled her as she saw Chaos smiling, flying low to the ground. Thankfully, she'd forgiven her for excluding her from the danger in Fairfield Castle. She still pretended she didn't understand Carissa's reasoning in trying to keep her safe, but Cari knew that she did. They were understanding each other much better now.

What Carissa didn't understand was why Hiya always had to cause a ruckus no matter where he went. She frowned seeing Cynth accidentally bump into Hiya while trying to keep the dress unwrinkled in her hands behind him. Hiya slowed and then used his shoulder to bump right back into Cynthia, causing her to drop the hem of the dress altogether. Hiya let go and launched into a full fighting match with Cynth. Though still low to the floor, the two hovered in the air, hands on each other's shoulders, pushing and pulling and kicking at one another.

Carissa cleared her throat a little too loudly. She lifted her head and narrowed her eyes to give them a sharp look. The two let go, turned red, and flew forward to grab the train of the dress again. Hela looked at Carissa worriedly, and the apothecary smiled reassuringly so as not to arouse any distress in the bride. Hela's expression relaxed, and she returned her gaze ahead to the groom. Cari's smile became real again, and gladness swelled in her heart as she saw the joy on Hela's face increasing with every step.

While the bride was a vision, Carissa couldn't help but catch a glance of Varick lurking in the background. Carissa frowned. Instead of taking a seat, of which there were plenty, he'd chosen to separate himself from the rest of the wedding guests to stand and sulk by the door to the reception hall, which was Fen's new estate and every bit as glorious, if not more so than Hela's father's home.

Before breaking her gaze from the sidhe back to the bride, there was a moment, perhaps imagined, in which she saw Varick looking not at Hela, but at someone in the rows of chairs behind Carissa. She turned and looked, catching sight of Jane, who was also looking at the sidhe instead of the bride. Cam must have seen it too because the two looked at each other in shock. The bride passed them, and they turned back around in their seats.

"You don't think?" Carissa asked.

"Nah," Cam said. "Varick and Jane? I don't think so."

"Shh!" Sal hushed them. "It's starting." The pair quieted. Hela and Fen held hands and smiled like two people without a care in the world.

The reverend began, "Dearly beloved...."

It was a perfect wedding. They'd opted out of reciting their own vows, especially after the cost of Fen's last creative ventures, but the look in their eyes said enough by itself. When all was over, the fae and humans all danced the night away. Spotting Maren alone at a table eating an unreasonably large slice of cake, Carissa took a seat beside her friend.

"How are you holding up?" Cari asked.

Maren's eyes were shining. She wasn't quite crying, but not quite all right. "They have cake," she said with an edge that added the silent declaration that there was no telling what Maren might have done had they not had said cake. Cari put a hand on Maren's shoulder. There were no words to make her feel better. Or, if there were, Carissa couldn't think of them.

"You know," Maren said, "I liked him. Of course, I should've probably realized he was a hobgoblin, no one's that perfect." Maren stuffed a giant piece of the Gooseberry Delight into her mouth. Carissa slid the elderberry wine in the opposite direction from her friend.

"One day," Cari said, "you'll find someone who might not be perfect, but he'll be perfect for you. Who knows? He might even turn out not to be a hobgoblin." Cari gave her a teasing smile before picking up a fork and attacking a piece of cake herself.

Maren sighed. "Well, that's easy for you to say. You've got Cam—don't give me that look. He's head over heels for you. Even that one guy who saved your life is over there looking at you right now," Maren said it casually and finished her slice. Carissa looked up to see Alden all the way at the other end of the garden. She was surprised Maren had seen him all the way over by the hedges. Her vigilance must have increased since the shock of John's betrayal. Alden was, in fact, looking in their direction. "If you're going to go over there, can I have your piece?" Maren pointed at the sugar-frosted slice on Carissa's plate.

Cari nodded. She still hadn't told Maren about Alden. Being friends with an ankou was one thing. That the ankou was an old classmate was another entirely. Maren had been through enough shock already.

Carissa walked all the way to the edge of the garden where a little stone ledge separated the backyard from a path leading back to the rest of the village. Chaos's chocolate cosmos sat there. She'd placed it there at the beginning of the ceremony. As much as Cari tried to wean her off it, Chaos was still attached to the plant and wouldn't leave home without it. Now, Alden stood beside it, as if keeping guard.

Alden's gaze shifted as she approached. His skin was still transparent at certain angles, something she had been sure she would never get used to. It didn't bother her anymore, though. His presence didn't scare her in the way it had the very first night she'd seen him as the ankou. His eyes rested on her a moment, but then returned to the party.

"Why not join them?" Carissa asked softly.

"It would scare them."

"Not all of them. Jane would be happy to see you." He turned his face to Carissa, who could see the full skeleton appear and fade in an instant.

"Not like this," he said. She didn't argue. She wasn't sure how she would feel if she were him. It must have been hard for him to watch over everyone he loved but stay in the background. She could understand him not wanting them to see what he'd become. She would have told him that Jane wouldn't care about his being ankou, that she'd only be happy to see her brother again, but Carissa knew Alden understood that himself. Instead, she changed the subject.

"I'm not sure I said a proper thank you for saving my life. Teaming with the sidhe to stop John, it was brave of you. I think all of Moss Hill would offer you their gratitude if they could, so I'll say it for all of us: thank you."

Alden looked at her for a long time. Whether he was at a loss for words, emotional, or just couldn't think of what to say was anyone's guess, but at long last, he nodded.

"There you are." Cameron left the partygoers to walk over to them. "Alden!" Cam paused. "I see you've dressed for the occasion." He glanced up and down at the ankou's attire: the constant black cloak and clothing befitting a reaper of death.

"Ha-ha," Alden said wryly, but he followed it with a faint smile.

"Lovely wedding, wasn't it?" Cam asked. "Makes you think, you know, about feelings, and people, and people who have feelings for people," he rambled.

Alden frowned and looked away. "I should go." The ankou faded from sight. Carissa hit Cam lightly on the shoulder.

"Ow, what?" Cam complained.

"You made Alden leave."

"Did I?" Cam appeared genuinely dumbfounded.

"Yes, with all your personal talk about feelings. He thought you wanted a private moment with me."

Cam looked thoughtful for a minute. Then, as if to himself, he said, "I wonder…. I think maybe he left for a different reason."

"What's that?" Carissa asked. But Cam didn't answer. Instead, he hopped up on to the brick wall beside her. "Hey, look at that." He pointed to the chocolate cosmos. "Full bloom. Must be the end of summer."

Carissa looked at it absently. Her eyes wandered from the flower to the party. She wasn't thinking any profoundly deep thoughts, but she was content in the moment. Cameron cleared his throat.

"Quite a risk Alden was willing to take with the sidhe," Cam remarked, jogging her out of her thoughts.

She breathed deep. "I know," she said. "It shows how much he loves Moss Hill, that he'd go that far protect it."

"Is that what you think?" Cam asked. He was looking at her like there was something she should already know.

"What?" she asked.

"You think it was Moss Hill he was protecting?"

"And Jane, his family, and friends," she added.

"You really don't get it, do you?"

"Get what?"

He laughed. "You always underestimate how much people are willing to do for you, Carissa Shae."

With that, Cameron hopped off the wall and dusted off his pant legs.

She scoffed. "He saved you, too!"

"Oh, I didn't say he didn't love me too." He grinned his goofy grin. Then, he extended his arm gallantly for her to take. "Care for a moonlit walk?"

Carissa took his offer. She felt a strange flutter in her chest as she reached toward him. It must have been the pure happiness of the occasion. The two strolled arm in arm down a lane, basking in the glow of the budding flower on a joyful summer eve.

Sneak Peek of Book 2: Remedy and Ruins

Summary: *Carissa Shae, half-elf/half-human apothecary, has been through some harrowing events this year. With the October All Hallows Eve celebration coming up, her friends use the festivities as a way to lift her spirits. They've volunteered, along with several Moss Hill residents, to decorate the old ruins of Fairfield Castle as a haunted house, and they've elected Carissa to spearhead the project. Reluctantly, she accepts the position, but regrets it immediately when a tragic accident occurs on the castle grounds. When foul play is suspected, fear threatens to cancel the celebrations. Can Carissa remedy the situation in time for the holiday?*

The pumpkin spiced tea warmed Carissa Shae to her core. She pulled her long sleeves over her thumbs and cradled the cup in her hands, relishing the heat. Her pink nose made her hair seem redder and the orange sweater didn't help.

The contrast of the crisp fall weather and the steamy holiday tea invited her to stay in the garden a little longer. From her seat on the patio, she had a perfect view of Mount Vale, the most mysterious feature of Moss Hill. Mysterious, that is, to any human who was not half-fae. All Mossies, as the residents of Moss Hill referred to themselves, knew that the west mountain was home to elves and sidhe and several other kinds of faerie people, yet being human and most never having seen it, they were still distant enough to it to view it with awe. Yet, at the right time, in the right season, at just the right angle, walking through the forest up the mountain could lead to the Otherworld.

Today fit those conditions perfectly.

Want more great content?

Hi, I'm Astoria Wright, the author of The Faerie Apothecary Cozy Mysteries. I hope you've enjoyed the first book in this series.

Check out the rest of
The Faerie Apothecary Mysteries:
Available on Amazon

Chaos in the Countryside
Herbs and Homicide
Remedy and Ruins
Elixirs and Elves
Charms and Changelings
Potions and Panic
Talismans and Turmoil
Tonics and Turning Points

To keep up to date about this series and others by the author, check out the website:

www.astoriawright.com

Sign up for the mailing list for updates and freebies available only to members!

A Note from Chaos:

Do you like this book?
I hope you do.
Please do me a favor
and leave a review!

Thanks for reading!

www.ingramcontent.com/pod-product-compliance
Lightning Source LLC
Chambersburg PA
CBHW022057170626
46808CB00002B/482